Bones in the Schrank

Bones in the Schrank

Joyce Holland

Copyright © 2009 by Joyce Holland.

Library of Congress Control Number: 2009904178
ISBN: Hardcover   978-1-4415-3274-9
              Softcover   978-1-4415-3273-2

All rights reserved. No part of this book may be reproduced or transmitted in any form or by any means, electronic or mechanical, including photocopying, recording, or by any information storage and retrieval system, without permission in writing from the copyright owner.

This is a work of fiction. Names, characters, places and incidents either are the product of the author's imagination or are used fictitiously, and any resemblance to any actual persons, living or dead, events, or locales is entirely coincidental.

This book was printed in the United States of America.

To order additional copies of this book, contact:
Xlibris Corporation
1-888-795-4274
www.Xlibris.com
Orders@Xlibris.com

For

Family, Friends, and Colleagues

Prologue

Berlin, Germany 1988

Justin filled out the forms required for crossing, turned over his ID card, and exited the room. He walked along the small porch of the guard shack and down the stairs. Once in the car, he drove slowly towards the opening in the Wall under the alert eyes of guards in the watch tower.

YOU ARE LEAVING
THE AMERICAN SECTOR

Justin hardly noticed the sign in four languages as he drove across the divide at Checkpoint Charlie separating the American and Russian sectors. An East German soldier in drab brown uniform pointed to a parking space near the passport inspection office and gestured to Justin to get out. While he was inside, a search would be made of his 1980 Mercedes.

By now, the routine was familiar although no less tedious, but Justin remembered the first time when it was new and daunting. In the early seventies conditions always seemed tense between the Allies and Russia, especially over Berlin. As he walked up wooden steps to the office, the station commander emerged from a side door and their eyes met. The indifferent officer looked away and passed Justin without a word.

Once inside, Justin began the process of presenting his documents and changing the obligatory 25 D-marks for the same amount of the East German currency. The dim room was stuffy and overheated in contrast to the cold winter day outside.

The line stagnated, as it always did. The East Germans were more bureaucratic than their cousins in the West, if that were possible, he thought, but Justin knew from experience that the process was intended to exasperate as well as intimidate. By now, it was just to be endured.

The bored soldier working behind the wire cage sent Justin's passport to a back room for review while another searched the bag of rationed goods Justin was carrying to his mother-in-law: coffee, salami, wurst, personal items hard or impossible to acquire in the long lines at the local stores in Louisa's neighborhood.

Justin looked around at others in line and knew from their collective torpor look that most of them were familiar with the process as they let it play out. The only impatient ones were the two or three American tourists, obviously new to the experience, and contemptuous of the indignity of having to wait. And wait some more.

"*Alles ist OK, Ja?*" Justin smiled at the soldier.

The soldier, barely looking at him, replied, "*Ja,*" and pointed to an area near a door where Justin was to wait for his passport and bag.

Once again in his vehicle, finally cleared, Justin drove slowly across the buffer zone behind the Wall, and down Friedrichstrasse. Shabby, dank, dark, the Eastern zone began with buildings facing no-man's land, their windows boarded shut, their grim rooms uninhabited. Every building along Friedrichstrasse was black with decades of accumulated dirt. Some were scorched by the fires caused by bombs; the facades were chipped from blasts and still showed bullet holes from the street fighting when the Russians had captured Berlin at the end of World War II.

Justin knew he was near the Berliner Ensemble Theater where Brecht had produced his plays and which had continued as a thriving theater after the playwright's death. He'd never been a fan, but Anna, his Anna, was. One night early in their marriage, they crossed over to meet Anna's mother and younger brother for a production of *Mother Courage*. It had been difficult. Being German, Anna had to enter by the Friedrichstrasse U Bahn station and he through Checkpoint Charlie. The occasion was disturbing for Anna since she had left East Berlin years earlier before the Wall. There were bad memories of living there after the war, and she feared she might be arrested. They didn't cross over together again. He always thought of that evening when driving the route.

It was a winter Saturday afternoon. The tour buses pulled to the curbside blocking vehicles, and the passengers, spilling to the street, were tying up traffic as they meandered through passing cars along the avenue. He turned right and proceeded down Prenzlaur Promenade and towards a residential area farther out from the city center. Lousia still lived in the house where her husband had moved the family late in the war. He had insisted at the time it was safer from the bombing than where they were living in Charlottenburg. A son, Albert, and his family lived further out.

The garage was one of a group at the end of the block. Justin pulled inside while thinking: this is the last time. His instincts told him it had become too risky. *We've maxed. I don't care what Peter says. The money's just not worth it.* Gathering up his parcels, he closed the garage door behind and walked into the gray afternoon.

Louisa put on a kettle for coffee. "I made some strudel for you." She pointed to the plate on the table. Dressed in a faded jumper house dress covered by a sweater, her silver gray hair framed an aristocratic face.

"You always do." Justin laughed. "I look forward to it, but here, I brought some coffee in my pocket for my visit." Justin pulled a small pouch from his pocket. "I know you share with Albert the provisions I bring. And, look, I also brought some pictures of the boys. Phillip will graduate this spring. He's been admitted to Cornell in New York!" *The one I flunked out of,* Justin added to himself. He admired Anna's mother who might have left East Berlin when she reached retirement age, but by staying was able to share with and assist her younger son and his family who lived nearby.

After the visit, Justin retraced his route and passed once more through East German control, dropping a few unused DDR marks in the Red Cross distribution box. His Mercedes received the usual 'mirrors under car' routine, but only a cursory search of his trunk and interior. *Karl's done his job again.* Justin quietly exhaled in relief. This was the part he always sweated. It was hard for him to look uninterested and guiltless. He passed through American control, picked up his ID and other checked items, and drove through a darkening afternoon to the Dahlem apartment.

Monday morning Justin was drawn quickly aside and bombarded with excited questions from Ralph, one of the British car agents operating with the Exchange. "Did you hear about Peter? His home was raided, and the garage found with all sorts of electronics, and he was picked up carrying thousands of D-marks. The police say he was black marketing."

"No! When? Which police? Who picked him up?"

Ralph had little to add. He heard it from a friend over in the British sector that morning. Justin was stunned. What happened? Would he also be arrested? Frightened and alarmed, he went to his office at the rear of the PX. He mustn't panic, he told himself. Play everything normal. Yet it took almost thirty minutes before his racing heart slowed down and his breathing was regular.

By lunch time, no officials, military or civilian, had approached him. With Peter no longer available to handle a transfer, he decided he would remove the package from the car and stash it. He didn't know who, if anyone would come for it. He didn't want to leave it in his Mercedes.

On the way out, Justin purchased a small travel bag. Once in the garage behind his apartment, it took about ten minutes for him to remove the package, place it in the bag, and restore the hidden compartment. Carrying the bag, he walked a few blocks to the U Bahn. Downtown, near KaDeWe, he rented a locker in a health club and deposited the bag. It was a businessmen's club he used on occasion, and he was not unknown.

Justin was away from work for over two hours, but no one seemed to notice or care. The rest of the day went without incident. No one said anything to him about Peter, which he took as a good sign. Peter wasn't known to many on the American base, nor in the Exchange. Only a couple of Brits were aware of their casual acquaintance. Outside the gate to the base, Justin flagged a cab to take him home. He had missed lunch and was hungry.

Anna and the boys weren't home yet. Justin poured a scotch and retreated to his den sanctuary. He tried to relax and found it hard. Sooner or later someone would come looking for the package. He didn't like to think who that might be. Politzei? MPs? Peter's friends? His heart raced. He started at a sudden loud noise on the street. His thoughts were chaotic. *How do I get rid of it?*

Chapter One

McLean, VA. 1999

Justin took the call in his study one Sunday afternoon in mid October. The Redskins had just defeated the Dallas Cowboys, and he was jubilant. "Justin here."

It took a moment for him to register when he heard who was calling. "Peter? Peter? I can't quite recall." He listened. "Peter Dominique? Peter!" Justin felt a surge of surprise, and something akin to panic. "How the hell are you?"

"And how are you, Justin my old buddy?" an accented voice replied. "Are you surprised to hear it's me?"

"Yes. Yes, I am." Justin responded. "Where in the hell are you? *Peter? My God. It can't be.*

"Right now, New York. I know you're in D.C., but New York is as far as I'm traveling. I live in Toronto now and am down on business, as you Yanks say. I was told you'd expect me to call."

Justin felt his stomach turn over his Budweiser and chips. "Not really. I haven't been expecting anything, but it's good to hear your voice again," Justin lied. "How have you been? How long have you been back in Canada?" *What should I say? Peter, Jesus!*

"You mean when did I get out of Mannheim Prison," Peter asked in a tense harsh voice. "They released me a couple of years ago and deported me home as I came out the door."

Justin paled under his golfer's tan. He felt his heart beat quicken. "I was really shocked at what happened to you. Do you know who tipped?

How did it come down? It must have been grim." What did Peter expect him to say?

"I appreciate what it must have meant to you." Justin heard the sarcasm. "And I've supposed all these years what it meant that I never involved you. Yeah man, it was living Hell. Worse than you ever heard." Peter was sitting on the bed in a motel near LaGuardia Airport while he made the call. Across the room, another man sat silently listening to one side of the conversation. Peter frowned at him and mouthed an obscenity.

Momentarily speechless, Justin finally answered. "My God."

After exchanging a few more guarded words the wiry French Canadian pushed the button. "I expect you know why I'm calling. We really need to cut the shit." Justin didn't respond. The other man in the motel room nodded urging Peter on. "I know you spoke to Karl not long ago in Dresden. You need to come to New York where we can enjoy a fond reunion and talk."

"Talk? Talk about what? I told Karl what happened. What are you saying?"

"Ha! Don't give me shit. Don't you want to see your old colleague? Really! You need to hear how a few years in Mannheim make a real man of a man."

"Peter . . ." Justin trailed off.

"Come on. Come on. It'll be like old times, and we do need to talk over old times." Peter smirked at the other man who had raised his eyebrows, but did not smile. His face was inscrutable.

Justin's alarm rose at the implied threat. "Look, Peter, my wife and I have plans for this coming weekend. We're going Thursday. How about next week? I'd like to see you, but there's really nothing to say about old times. I'm sorry for what happened to you, but those days are long gone." He laughed lightly, "I can't disappoint my Frau, you know, and I have to go to work some of the time." Justin wondered if Peter knew Anna and he had divorced.

"No, tomorrow or Tuesday. I can't spend more time here this trip. Change your plans. We have things to talk about." Peter was emphatic. "My old friends are very interested in you now that you've surfaced, and sent me for the interview."

Surfaced. That's a crock. You mean screwed. Justin hit the desk with a fist, and then surrendered with as much grace as he could muster trying not to react to Peter's message. "Well, Jackie's going to be pissed, to put it mildly, but I'll see what can be done. By the way, I'm no longer with Anna. Have a new wife."

Justin gathered his thoughts and not waiting for a reaction to his news said, "Look, I'll try to get things changed and be up at the Pierre by Tuesday evening. Call me there about six to see if I made it. Otherwise, it'll be Wednesday. Give me a number to call. I don't know how easily I can work it out on this short notice. I know a restaurant where we can quietly talk over old times," he parroted Peter. *I can't believe this. God!* Justin's thoughts raced. Perspiration wet his forehead.

"That sounds more like what I had in mind. But make it Tuesday. I can't stay here forever. Good talking to you, friend. Ciao."

Justin thought he might puke. So much for the Denver game. *What the hell am I going to do now? Shit. What do I tell Jackie?* Justin switched off the muted TV and put on a jacket. He needed to get out of the house and think.

On Tuesday, Justin took a shuttle from National and a cab from LaGuardia into the city. He was in the hotel by five. Changing weekend plans had not been easy, and Jackie was more than miffed. They were able to reschedule their long weekend and, as a sweetener to appease her, he suggested that Jackie's brother and his wife come along as guests. He went into the office Monday morning, rescheduled appointments, and by Tuesday morning had made arrangements. All the while, he was thinking about how he was going to handle the meeting with Peter.

It was clear to Justin that Karl and acquaintances had not bought his story. No question about that. But why, after all this time, were they suspecting him for the lost delivery? He'd been a bit player, a write-in aside from the other activities he and Peter had shared. Yes, he'd been part of black marketing, but the drug thing? No. He was involved only because he made those visits to Louisa. Often he looked back and thought what a fool he was to have been sucked in, but still the payoff had been sweet. Too much to resist. But after more than ten years! A lifetime ago in Germany. Who are they, he kept thinking? Why come after him now?

The receptionist greeted Justin. "Nice to see you back, Mr. Lawrence."

"I appreciate the accommodation on such short notice."

"We always have room for you, Mr. Lawrence," he said, handing Justin the key and motioning to the bell captain. "And if you need to stay longer, just let us know." Justin smiled his thanks, and turned from the desk.

Once in his room, Jus saw the call button blinking on his phone. He ignored it at first and quickly unpacked, putting his toiletries in the bathroom. He opened the mini bar and poured himself a Scotch. He spread the curtains and gazed out across Central Park and at the rush hour traffic far below. It already was dark and the city lights were aglow. New York. His home.

Justin was angry that he had given in to make the trip. Angry, while also alarmed. The encounter with Karl in September still bothered him, and although he managed to suppress it, the anxiety he had felt at the time resurfaced. And how would the outcome of this meeting with Peter impact his relationship with Jackie? Justin continued to gaze out over the city.

Angry and humiliated by the IG investigation into theft of merchandise from the Berlin Post Exchange inventory and of Justin's possible involvement, Anna divorced him when he left AAFES, refusing to leave Berlin. Justin still remembered how upset and distressed he had been, and how long it took to get over losing her. Later, he lied to Jackie about the investigation, telling her he was not guilty just as he had Anna, pointing out that he was cleared of the charges. As for the drugs, even Anna didn't know. Was his past catching up with him again?

Justin turned reluctantly to the phone and dialed for messages. Peter had left a number to call only minutes before he checked in. *Early, the bastard.* After a hesitation, Jus called.

"I'm calling for Peter. This is Justin."

"Here."

"Peter? I'm in my hotel."

"Wonderful. I knew you could do it."

"Yeah." Justin sipped his drink. "It's been a hassle. I wish you could have waited until next week."

"No way. I can't stay forever."

"I'm here. So look, let's move on. There's a small restaurant on East 83rd St., Gasthaus Europa. I'll call and have them reserve us a back table. I've gone there for years. Meet you around seven?"

"Why not your hotel?"

"We have to eat, and we want somewhere we can relax and not be bothered. We haven't seen each other for some time. And you say there's something special to talk about."

"You know exactly what we have to talk about."

"This place has good legit German food," Justin ignored Peter's reply. "Hard to find any more. Schwabisch owner. You up for that? On me."

"I don't know. I haven't really eaten much real German for a long time. Only the crap they served in Mannheim. How about a pizza in your room?"

Justin rolled his eyes and shook his head. "Oh come on. I know the place. It's nothing posh, and the beer's good." He fell easily into talking to Peter as in the earlier days, casual and unceremonious. He was going to be upbeat and convincing with Peter. Justin was on the verge of panic by the turn of events, but he would stick to his story: He hadn't taken the package, but someone came for it and trashed his car. He had to be convincing. He didn't want to be alone with Peter. *I wonder if someone's with him.* Familiar surroundings would help.

"All right, I guess it's as good as anywhere. What's the address again?"

A short time later Justin got out of the cab a block from the restaurant. He wanted a few minutes to prepare himself. A drizzle wet the pavement reflecting the streetlights and those from moving cars. He liked the feel of the moisture on his face in spite of the cold. It had a calming effect. The area had changed greatly since the Forties when he was a child, but it still evoked strong memories.

At first, his mother had come in from Brooklyn with him and his brother, as his grandmother walked them through the "Germantown" of Manhattan, looking in shop windows, listening to the people on the street greet one another and passing the time of day. His Oma still knew friends here and children of friends, from the time she and Opa first arrived in New York before World War I. They lived on the block until success in business led them to move to Brooklyn. Later, when Justin and Johan were older, the two came with her alone. Sometimes, a cousin or two would join them, but Justin and Johnny were Oma's favorites.

She lived with them in what had been her house in Brooklyn and continually spoke to them in German, determined they would use the language. She never learned English that well anyway. It was something they alternately appreciated and resented, but there was no question they loved their Oma. They would end up at one of the Konditori, and have a cake with cocoa while the adults had coffee. Often, some acquaintances from the neighborhood would join them while the chatter went on in a mix of English and German. It was a good time for Justin.

Across the smallish room near the back of the restaurant, Peter already was seated. Justin spotted him at once when he entered. Peter motioned to him. Justin waved and spoke to the man at the register.

"It's been awhile. Good to see you, Al."

"Same here. Is this a special occasion?"

"An old acquaintance I haven't seen in awhile. I wanted to treat him to a good meal."

"I'm glad you came. The neighborhood changes, but the place keeps going."

"You're a city landmark. Did you notice if anyone came in with him?" Justin probed. He was certain Peter was a go-between.

"I think he was alone. Are you expecting anyone else?"

Justin shook his head. "No, but I thought he might bring along a buddy."

"I'll keep my eye out." Al nodded, sensing there was more to Justin's meeting than he let on. "Enjoy your meal."

They laughed and Justin walked over to join his former collaborator. Peter didn't get up, but Jus reached across the table and offered his hand. "Good to see you again," he lied.

"Good to see you." Peter responded as they shook hands. Justin was taken back by the change in him.

In Berlin, Peter had been upbeat, flippant, and irreverent. He was always on the make: young and confident. Cheerful and wise-cracking, Peter was never quiet for long. He believed the Establishment—West German and Allies—was preoccupied by the political hoopla, and he operated with contempt of its ability to catch him. He also was careful and shrewd. Because of these characteristics, Justin wondered how Peter had been compromised and arrested. Probably betrayed by rivals he once concluded.

The man who sat before him was a different individual. His eyes were almost expressionless and did not reflect the small smile he had shown when exchanging greetings. His face revealed a hardness that had not been there before, and his personality was now subdued. Yet his body seemed to be coiled ready to spring, suggesting a dangerously shrouded fire was lurking. Angry, broken, or desperate, Justin wondered? Or all three?

A waiter brought a beer for each to the table, and they ordered. "Prost," Justin offered.

Peter clinked glasses and gave Justin a veiled look. "Cheers."

They exchanged some small talk and Justin told a little of his time in the area in his youth. "Opa was a good businessman, and Oma was a dear and wonderful person." Justin concluded his brief reminiscence. "My dad and uncle worked in the store while growing up, and took over when they finished college. The store grew and grew. Later, they sold it to a chain. My uncle took his share and moved to D.C. where he started building his dealership. That's where I ended up when I left AAFES."

Peter listened quietly while Justin rattled on. "Why did you leave your job if you were cleared of the charges? You were lucky about that, weren't you? I thought they would get us both for sure." The Canadian spoke frankly, showing little emotion. Justin wondered if Peter believed he had tipped off the IG to draw suspicion away from himself.

"They had come too close to proving my involvement, and I didn't think it a good idea to go back to Berlin. When my uncle offered me the opportunity to come in with him, I jumped at it." Justin purposely avoided mentioning his later acquisition of Uncle Wilhelm's franchise.

He didn't want Peter to know how much he was worth. "The decision lost me Anna, and that part was hard to get over. How have things gone with you?" Justin probed for a connection between Karl's contacts in Dresden and Peter's in Toronto.

Peter shifted restlessly. "It hasn't been easy. I didn't think it a good idea to go back to Quebec, so I chose Toronto which isn't so close-knit. You know what I mean?" Justin wasn't sure he did. "But there's not much there either for an ex-con, and all I can get is a few odd jobs. I have some part time work at the Air Canada Center arena working with concessions and clean up. Stuff like that. That's when the Maple Leafs are in season." Angry at his situation, Peter hit the table with his fist and shook his head in disgust.

The first of their meal arrived, and the waiter set down a second beer for both. When he left, Peter changed the subject, "You know why we're here. It's time we discuss unfinished business."

"I'm not exactly sure why we're here," Justin replied, "but I guess from my conversation with Karl that someone believes I cashed in the delivery I brought out the day you were arrested. Maybe also had a hand in the tip to the German police."

"I think I've convinced the 'someones' that you would have been a fool to be involved with fingering me. You were too close to the deals we had going with the receivers of our merchandise to draw attention to yourself. We already thought some kind of IG or AAFES investigation was underway anyway. I never thought you turned on me, but if they got me, they should have been close to you." Peter's tone was bitter.

Alarmed by Peter's vehemence, Justin answered, "Believe me, I sweated. After you were taken in, I was questioned three or four times, and eventually I was put on administrative leave. As we suspected, a full investigation was well under way. I finally was transferred out of Berlin to Headquarters in Dallas while they tried to wrap it up. In the end two or three of the military guys working part time were indicted, and one of the other managers. Even a teacher, if you can believe it, was caught. Although they tried to prove I was stealing from the inventory, they couldn't nail me, so I was cleared. That's when I got out. Lucky you and I dealt direct. I don't know how they got onto you," he concluded. "Maybe someone in the Brit exchange, or one of your German contacts."

"I think I know who it was, but that doesn't matter anymore. There were no drugs on me, and they found only a trace in my place. There wasn't much of a case on drugs, so they raised my sentence for the rest: stolen goods, black-marketing. They said I was transporting D-marks to the East, the fools. They arrested me with the payment for the delivery you brought out. What crap."

Justin was startled by the fierceness of Peter's contempt over the prosecution. "I know how you feel. I was glad my case wasn't being pursued by the Germans."

"Anyway," Peter went on, "I convinced my contacts that it wasn't you who was responsible for my arrest. At the same time, I don't know that you didn't unload the delivery yourself. They seem to believe you did. The street value was well over three million, maybe four, though not what they were getting. It was good stuff. They think they are due a payoff since the payment was seized by the Politzi before I could hand it over. Plus a little extra for the inconvenience." He glared at Justin and tapped the table for emphasis.

Justin ate his meal absorbing what he heard and considered his next response. Peter's story about his arrest and trial closely matched what had been reported at the time, except for the part about drugs. Without the evidence of drug dealing, the conviction concentrated on what Peter said it did. Now Jus understood why he had not been investigated over the drug transports. The police didn't know, and Peter wisely kept his mouth shut.

So who are they? Can the group Peter and Karl were connected with could still be viable? Or is it some offshoot gang, or subgroup, or clone or . . . ? He couldn't imagine. It seemed so preposterous.

Justin didn't have any idea how the drug gangs operated, other than what he sometimes heard, read, or saw on TV. In Europe he had known a little from what was said by Peter and his German friends. Everyone knew the drug trade was a big item in Berlin. Justin also knew then the people involved were violent and dangerous, which was why he became more and more reluctant to continue making the trips through Checkpoint Charlie. As for now, he was aware that drug gangs were numerous in D.C., but his dealerships were mostly in the suburbs and so far not affected.

According to the *Washington Post* and local TV, the groups spent most of their violent energy against each other. People who bought out in the suburbs or drove into the city were seldom observed or hassled by the police. Most efforts were concentrated on the inner city and Anacostia. Justin was bothered by what Peter had said. *On what evidence, after all this time, could 'they' base their decision that I got rid of the delivery?*

More customers had come in; there was loud, boisterous laughter from one of the tables. A single man was seated at another not far from Justin and Peter.

Justin shook his head in puzzlement and broke the silence. "I don't understand why they think I'm the one who unloaded the package. When I saw the mess in our car, I thought for sure it was someone from your group that got it. Louisa, Anna's mother, told us that after my visit, two men came to her apartment and were pretty nasty with her. They asked how to find me in West Berlin and when she expected me back."

"That's all well 'n good but whatever happened, they've thought for a long time you somehow managed the deal. If anyone riffled your car, what they were looking for already was gone."

"It's not possible. The front seats were pulled away, sliced to bits, and the floorboard was ripped apart, the specially built compartment open and empty. It was the first time I saw where it was located." Justin leaned across the table and looked intently into Peter's eyes. "Part of the dash was ripped out, and the back seat messed up as well. I wasn't there when they concealed it in the car while I visited with Louisa. Even if I thought I could cash in with it, I tell you I didn't have a clue where to look. The whole thing is crazy."

"Of course you notified the Politzi about the car." Peter smirked with sarcasm, referring to the German police.

"Right. I couldn't even report it to my insurance. Anna was furious with me. I told her it happened on the street near Kerfurstendam. There was a demonstration a couple of blocks away that day. I said it was crazy for us to get the Berlin police and the MPs involved. It might have been an anti-American gang, or some other rad group, and we'd be stupid to draw attention to ourselves. My refusal to report it didn't fly very well. I paid the whole cost of repair myself. I think the incident added to Anna's growing unhappiness with me. As I said, when I decided to settle in the States, she refused to leave Berlin."

Peter nodded and with his mouth full asked, "Your new wife. She a looker? You always were casing out the ladies."

Justin ignored his comment knowing he was being taunted. "She's a great woman. Beautiful in many ways. Sister of an American I met skiing in Cortina. We reconnected a couple of years after the divorce."

"That's sort of how a lot of marriages go, isn't it?"

"Anna's living in the Berlin apartment, which was hers anyway. Brought her mother over to be with her after the Wall came down. My younger son, Matthias, went back also and is working in Frankfurt for an international company." Justin was relieved they had moved away from the discussion about the drugs. "He's doing well. He says he feels more European than American. It seems a lot of our kids who grow up over there feel the same way."

They talked some more about Jackie and the children, and Justin felt the earlier tension between them subside. Then Peter said, "Jus, I'm not happy about this. If I'd been in your spot, I would've done the same. Why not? I've been told you unloaded the stuff in Frankfurt. Your dealer spilled to somebody a year or so after it happened. I don't know how it came about, but the description and other details point to you, from what I've been told. They put it together again after Karl got in touch a month or so ago. I guess someone's got a long memory."

"Frankfurt! And just how did I get it all to Frankfurt from Berlin? Perhaps in a diplomatic pouch thanks to my high level State connections." Justin was sure Peter would miss the sarcasm.

"Figuring it out is not up to me. They knew where I was when I was in Mannheim, and apparently where I went when I got out. A couple of weeks ago someone decided I was perfect to make the contact to collect their money. That's how I can afford to be here." Justin wondered just how much Peter may be involved with drug activity in Toronto. The story of renewed connection sounded too pat. He shook his head as if to make sense of what he was hearing.

"Look Jus, this is the bottom line. They figured you're responsible for what happened to the delivery, and you're very well fixed to compensate the interested parties. They want a flat one million US dollars. They want delivery in cash, but are willing to take it in two payments. One right away, one in a couple of months. Denominations of one hundred bills or less. You're to bring it up in a week or so and hand it over to me. We'll make the final arrangements close to when you're due."

Justin could hardly contain his shock, but just as he was about to speak another course arrived. Peter was served an entrée featuring sauerbraten and Justin a kalbsteak covered in Zigeuner or gypsy sauce. This gave him a minute to compose himself. He sipped his beer and spoke to the waiter, "It looks excellent. Please tell the cook. He's an old friend."

As soon as the waiter moved out of range, Justin leaned closer and in a hushed angry voice said, "Peter, this is mad! You and your friends can't possibly think I unloaded the package, and certainly can't believe I can, or will just hand over that much cash on such flimsy stories to justify the demand. You've been out of circulation too long."

Peter backed away in his chair, "It's the message I've been sent to deliver." "Look. People here don't just go to their bank and ask for a withdrawal of half a mill in small bills. What kind of reading did you do in Mannheim? Heavy on spy novels and science fiction? Someone's really got you going."

Peter laughed outright, and looked buoyant for the first time that evening. "Well spoken my friend. I'll take that back to them." Justin wondered if Peter was reflecting the beer or relief.

"Come on Peter. Get real," he said. "What you're suggesting sounds like something out of *The French Connection*."

Peter chuckled again; his eyes were suddenly alight with merriment. "I can see your point, Jus, but maybe you should consider that you're the one out of touch, and what's being suggested is much closer to the real world and how things work. Do you think I could make this up all by myself? Or know what you are worth, and where to find you?"

Justin didn't respond and concentrated on his dinner. Peter began to eat with enthusiasm. They finished with apple strudel for old times sake. The tension that the meal began with had all but dissipated once more, and the two were chuckling over some long ago escapades they shared in Berlin. As Justin signaled for the bill, Peter said, "This turned out much better than I expected. It really has been good to see you after all this time."

Justin smiled trying to appear unconcerned. "You'll tell your friends they've got the wrong guy?"

"I certainly will. I can't be too encouraging about what they'll say, but I will tell them. Either me or someone else will be in touch." Peter pushed away from the table, and then leaned forward. "From a friend, I'd suggest you start working out how you'll get the first payment together. These guys are really not nice, if you want my opinion."

"I'm sure when you point out how ludicrous it is to finger me, they'll be more realistic. And when you think about it, you too." Justin felt chilled and his hands were clammy. *Will these people really go away?*

"I guess we'll just have to see but don't count on it too much. Just coming from an old buddy, you know."

Justin paid the check while Peter went to the men's room. Al said quietly, "A guy came in a little after you. Sat at a table close to you and your friend."

"The dark complexioned guy?"

"Yeah."

"Thanks, Al. And the meal was excellent as usual."

Justin and Peter parted at the door and turned in opposite directions in the cold drizzle. Justin walked a couple of blocks taut with tension and fear. His mind was racing. He reviewed the conversation with Peter and the demand for money. *It's so crazy!* He spotted a cruising cab and hailed it realizing that walking the streets in the area so late was not very safe.

Once back at the hotel Justin lounged in the dark nursing a scotch, mulling over the past few hours. Sleep came hard, and he woke the next morning exhausted.

Chapter Two

The sun glowing reddish on the horizon continued to rise above the water, not yet high enough to cause a glare. Leonidas, a Chesapeake Retriever, raced ahead of the jogger. A northerly wind was picking up. "Red sun in morning, sailors take warning," the old saying slipped into her thoughts as Alexis ran along the beach. A front was approaching, but it would be clear most of the day.

The phone was ringing when Alexis winded from her run came in the door. She grabbed the kitchen extension before the answer machine could kick in.

"Mason residence. Hello."

"Alexis?" Is that you? This is Jackie Lawrence."

Alexis was surprised. "Why Jackie, how are you? How are Justin and the kids?" The last time she talked to Jackie was at the memorial service for Lucas two years ago.

"That is why I'm calling. Our lawyer told me not to involve anyone, but . . ." There was a short hesitation. "Justin is missing. The police are looking for his van, but there's no indication he's had an accident. I don't think they're looking very hard. I'm frantic, and I need your help to find him and uncover what happened." Jackie stopped to take a breath.

"What do you mean missing?" Startled at the news, Alexis stretched the phone over to the coffee pot and poured herself a cup. "Are you calling from home?" She sat down at the table in her spacious kitchen preparing to hear what Justin was up to now.

Ignoring the question, Jackie continued. "It's part of that incident back in Dresden. I'm sure of it. Justin hasn't been himself since. And then the car accident . . ."

"Wait. Wait. What are you talking about? Slow down." Alexis felt a chill of alarm. She looked out at the protective dunes in front of the house, the now bright sky, and the ocean beyond. It was a sight that had always provided comfort.

The voice at the other end broke when Jackie asked, "Can you come up? It's very complicated. Justin's disappeared. I'm frightened and desperate. I need your help." Jackie went on without waiting for an answer. "He left for a hunting trip with friends in New York, but when he didn't come back I called Ron who was to go as well. But Ron said he hasn't heard from Justin since they decided in October not to go this year. It's been three weeks now and I don't know where he went or where he is. I haven't heard a word. The police haven't found a trace."

There was a silence. Alexis paused to collect her thoughts. What did Jackie mean her lawyer told her not to involve anyone? Why did Justin say he was going hunting when he wasn't? "Jackie, I'm so sorry to hear this. Have you notified the FBI, or any agencies besides the police?"

"I've tried to get both involved, but they say there's no indication of a crime so far, or it hasn't been long enough, or on and on. The New York police have a statewide alert out on the van, but there hasn't been a sign of it. Nothing here in Virginia or the D.C. area. Our lawyer hasn't been able to get much more either. I don't know what to do. I can hardly function at work. The children are upset and confused." Alexis could tell from the way Jackie was speaking she was having a difficult time controlling herself.

"Why are you calling me, Jackie? Of course, I'll do whatever I can, but I'm sure your mother and Philip are helping, and they're right there." Alexis doubted Jackie's mother, Patricia, would provide much help. The slightest problem always threw her into a panic. Still, Phillip, Jackie's stepson, was a mature thirty years-old and lived within a few miles.

"I want to hire you to find Justin." Jackie was direct. Alexis shook her head. *Oh no.* "You know him, you know us, and you and Lucas have been good at things like this."

Alexis shook her head again. She had continued with the small private investigation agency after Lucas's death, although she had handled only a few cases. She considered herself successful and qualified, but she knew she didn't want to get involved with Jackie's situation. There was too much history with Justin. Alexis didn't like him much as a person and didn't feel comfortable around him. She hesitated. "I appreciate you thinking of me, but aren't there agencies up there that would be a better choice?"

Jackie quickly responded. "I don't want anyone up here. Not many people here know he's missing. Most think he's away on business. Our lawyer thinks it's a bad idea to get anyone at all, although I'm not sure why." For an instance Jackie regained her composure and spoke with resolve. "I need you, and Philip will be the only other to know."

Alexis hesitated again. Lucas and Alexis had kept contact with the Lawrence couple although neither particularly liked Justin. Jackie was the younger sister of Lucas' best friend, Chris, and she had been included in skiing trips in Europe, and later in the U.S. after both men left the navy. Chris didn't like Justin either, but he was big brother and lovingly protective of Jackie. So after Jackie and Justin were married, the three couples continued to socialize together. Alexis believed Lucas would want her to go up and at least listen to what Jackie had to say.

"I will come up and listen to your concerns and see if I can suggest anything to help. I can tell you are very distressed. But before I do, there're a few things I need to take care of here." For one, arranging to leave the children, she thought. "I'll try to fly up to Dulles tomorrow. Give me some directions to your house. I'm not sure I remember." Alexis realized she couldn't get a clear understanding of the situation over the phone with Jackie so distraught.

"Oh thank you, Alexis. I'm at my wit's end, and I don't know what else to do. I don't know what to tell the children. They're frightened and confused, and miss their father. I really need you."

After taking directions to the Lawrence house, Alexis hung up the phone. She sat thoughtful for a few minutes going over once more her decision to go to Jackie. She wondered if it was wise to be dragged into the situation in spite of what she thought Lucas would expect. Knowing Justin, it might be a messy affair.

* * *

September 1999: Dresden, Germany

Karl couldn't believe his eyes. Was it Justin Lawrence? Here in the Rustkammer?

The museum security official began to follow the tourist through the long gallery, careful to keep a safe distance while trying to get a closer look. The American moved slowly through the exhibit, studying the collection of armor and weapons used throughout Saxony history. He stopped in front of a case displaying ornately tooled flint—lock pistols, and Karl took a closer look. The man was older, yes, and starting to gray, but it definitely was Justin Lawrence; the same nervous Justin Lawrence who smuggled drugs through Checkpoint Charlie during the Eighties. Here in Dresden. Astounding! Karl returned to the gallery entrance, and moved out of sight behind counters in the reception area. He spoke briefly to one of the guards and waited for Justin to leave the museum.

Twelve years earlier, Karl was a colonel in the East German military, assigned to administer checkpoints and guard stations at the Wall. Although he had his connections with the Russian "friends" as well as the much feared Stasi, he understood that he and his family were being watched while he maintained his post. Yet, he knew the system and believed he was covered as he worked with his drug contacts. Although not a Party member, he had been loyal and a good officer. His assignments and steady promotions reflected his effectiveness. Karl always had done what he needed to survive. He deserved his share of return out of the corrupt Party system. You didn't have to be a Believer to be effective. Or successful.

Shortly after Peter's arrest, Karl sought a transfer to Dresden, which was granted. That's where he was when the Wall came down. Later, he was decommissioned from the army and, using his connections, was appointed as head of security at the museum.

Karl watched as Justin headed for the exit and cautiously followed him. Possibly someone would pay for knowledge of the American's presence. He thought he knew who it may be. Outside at the bottom of the museum steps, Karl watched Justin join a stylishly dressed woman, several years younger than he, who was waiting quietly in the September sun. Karl saw her smile at Justin as he reached her. They chatted a moment, and the woman showed him some purchases from another museum. Together, they crossed the garden in the direction of the Semper Opera. Karl followed. When the couple reached the Tashenbergpalais Hotel, Karl waited several minutes to let them clear the lobby. Then he walked around to an employee entrance and went in to verify with the hotel manager what he believed he had just observed.

* * *

Maria was Alexis' housekeeper who worked at the house three times a week. She was a single parent from El Salvador legally in the country. Her daughter was eight, the same age as Rebecca. The children liked and appreciated the woman who was efficient and level headed, and they responded well when left with her for an occasional overnight. Alexis had no qualms about leaving Maria in charge for a short time, especially with

Travis nearby in the apartment. So shortly after Maria's arrival, Alexis and she worked out the arrangements for Maria to stay at the house while Alexis traveled to D.C. the next day.

"Don't let Luke and Becky take advantage of you. They are to go to bed at their usual time." Alexis knew her children sometimes could manipulate Maria into minor concessions to their expected behavior.

"Si. I know. If I think they are not doing right, I will call you." Maria nodded.

"That's right. I'll give you the phone number when you leave today. It also will be on my desk. And Travis will be here as well," she added. "You and Rosa stay in your regular room upstairs."

When Alexis left from Dare County airport the next morning, the weather was closing as expected, but she was briefed and planed to outrace it. Alexis loved to fly, and her Lear was one of the luxuries made possible by Lucas' inheritance. Owning it also offered flexibility for sudden trips.

Once in the air, Alexis thought back to the eighties when the two of them were in Europe and she and Lucas learned to fly. Later both qualified in jets. In the States after Lucas left the navy, they flew often. The flight to Dulles took little more than an hour.

By afternoon, Alexis and Jackie were settled in the living room of the Lawrence McLean, Virginia home. Jackie had coffee and snacks ready when Alexis arrived. Artificial gas logs burned warmly while a misty rain fell in the gloomy slate day beyond the windows.

"I really appreciate the fact that you came." Jackie's hands shook as she poured the coffee. "I wasn't sure you would now that Lucas is gone."

"I'm happy to come." Alexis wondered if Jackie had sensed how she felt about Justin. "And Lucas would have wanted me to. I'm not sure I'm the right person for the job you have in mind, but I'll certainly listen to what you have to say."

Jackie appeared uneasy. She shifted nervously in the chair. *I wonder if Jackie's having second thoughts about calling me.* "Tell me about Justin."

"I'm not sure just where to begin." Jackie's voice was halting. "I guess with his sudden trip to New York." Alexis sat quietly and prepared to listen, although she wondered why Jackie didn't start with the incident in Dresden first mentioned in the phone call.

"Shortly after we returned in September from our vacation in Germany, Justin went to New York to meet a former colleague from his Berlin days. He had never spoken of Peter, and I was a little put out by his decision to go. It was unexpected, and we had plans to spend a long weekend at Hot Springs." Jackie turned away and covered her eyes. Alexis sipped her coffee and waited for Jackie to regain her composure. She looked around the room admiring the tastefully chosen furnishings. These she credited to Jackie, the art history major. Coming in the foyer Alexis had noticed an elegant antique schrank, a German standing closet. Was this a piece contributed by Justin? If so, how had he pried it away from Anna?

Jackie was ready to continue her narration. "Justin said he had lost contact with his friend whom he assumed had remained in Europe. Now it turns out, Peter is back in Canada. Jus seemed anxious to see him again. He said Peter had phoned unexpectedly and would be in New York only a short time." Jackie continued thoughtfully. "It wasn't like him, but he does have friends and occasional business in New York, so I tried not to get too upset. I was angry, and he knew I was, but he went anyway." Alexis listened, becoming more intrigued.

"Jus was only gone two days, and when he returned, he seemed bothered and somewhat withdrawn. At the same time, he said it had been an enjoyable opportunity to see his friend again. I recall Jus saying they met in a little German restaurant in the East 80's and talked long into the evening."

Alexis, trying to put the new event into perspective interrupted. "You mentioned on the phone some incident in Germany, what was that about? Was Peter involved?" Alexis wondered once more what, if anything, Justin's trip to see Peter had to do with the incident in Dresden and Justin's disappearance.

"I'll tell you about that, but you see it was only a few days after the New York trip that the crash occurred," Jackie said, as if everything were obvious.

Alexis tried not to look surprised and made a closer scrutiny of her friend. She was having difficulty following the disjointed narrative. "Okay. So finish about Peter, and then tell me about the crash," she coaxed, masking her frustration. *This is bizarre!* Alexis shifted in the chair.

Sitting up straighter Jackie gathered herself while taking a deep breath. Although she knew Alexis understood her effort to remain in control, she realized she wasn't getting her story out convincingly. "Jus had a phone call late one evening soon after he returned from New York. He said it was Peter, calling from Canada, saying he enjoyed their meeting and hoped they could see one another again soon. Jus was so agitated by the call that he didn't come back to bed for a couple of hours. He even went outside to think, I guess, and walked around the yard."

Alexis leaned forward intently. "Is that something he did often?" She wondered why Justin was agitated by the call. And why did Peter call that late just to say he enjoyed their time together. Odd.

"Not really. He rarely went into the yard or even on the patio, especially not so late at night." Jackie managed a smile. "You know these neighborhoods. I was afraid someone would see him out there, think we had a prowler, and then we'd have a patrol car in the driveway checking out the house!" At this, Alexis smiled as well, imagining the scene.

"The next day was Saturday, thank goodness, and I didn't have to get the children off to school or day care. Justin fixed himself a late breakfast and said he had to go into the office for awhile. He looked terrible and wouldn't talk about the night before. He wasn't gone more than two or three hours, and he seemed relieved when he came back." Jackie looked out the window. The sky had grown dark and ominous, and the icy rain was turning to snow. Alexis, thinking the weather matched the mood of the story, waited quietly for her friend to continue.

"That evening, we drove into town and met some friends for dinner and a performance at the Center. Justin was relaxed, his regular self, although from time to time he tuned out of the conversation and I sensed that he was bothered by the call from the night before. Then, on the way home, we were on the GW Parkway near the Ft. Marcy pull off. A car drove up close to our rear and bumped us. Jus tried to speed up as he struggled to keep control, but the car pulled around ours, sideswiped us, and sent us crashing onto the shoulder." Jackie shuddered at the memory.

Alexis frowned as she imagined the scene, and reached over the table to squeeze Jackie's hand. "Were you badly hurt?"

"I was hospitalized overnight, and Justin was badly bruised. The police said it looked like a drunken hit and run, but Jus didn't agree. He seemed full of remorse and guilt, as if he were somehow responsible. While waiting for the ambulance, he held me and said over and over, "Those bastards. I didn't believe they'd do something like this. I'm sorry. I'm so sorry."

* * *

November: McLean, Virginia

The morning after his return from New York, Justin left for the office early. He was thoughtful and disturbed. He wasn't sure how he was going to respond to Peter's demand for money. He tried to concentrate on his work.

Before going to his desk, he asked his secretary to reschedule a business luncheon. Later, he discussed several reports with Phillip and the general manager. He checked on his investments and placed a call to his broker. In late afternoon, Justin called his attorney. Louis also was the attorney for Justin's uncle. He had been connected to the family for years.

"Hello, Justin. How are you? I haven't heard from you for months. Was your trip to Germany a good one?"

"The trip was great. Jackie loved the museums in Prague and Dresden." He tried to sound cordial. "But I have a problem now that I need to discuss with you. It's serious, and I need your advice. Do you think we could meet at the club on Sunday and talk privately?"

"A problem? Business?"

"It's something else. Something that has come up recently. I'd rather not discuss it on the phone." Justin nervously shook his head and frowned.

"I'm sorry to hear it, Jus." Louis heard the anxiety in Justin's voice and took the cue not to press. "Jan and I have nothing special planned. Do you want to meet me for lunch about twelve thirty?"

Justin was relieved. "That will work. Thanks. That sounds perfect."

"Not at all. Try not to worry too much. I'll see you then."

After the call, Justin went home. He was exhausted and realized he had been tense all day in spite of his efforts to avoid thinking about the meeting with Peter. He would like to discuss the situation with Louis sooner. Sunday seemed a long time off.

Late Friday night a ringing phone woke Justin from deep sleep. Cursing, he picked up the bedroom connection. It was Peter calling from Toronto.

"How're things going?"

"What do you want? Do you know what time it is?"

"Just calling to see if you made it back okay."

Justin grabbed for his robe on the chair, "Look, my wife is asleep. Hold on while I go downstairs."

"Who is it?" Jackie asked.

"I'm taking it downstairs. Go back to sleep."

Half a minute later, seated at his desk, Justin resumed the conversation. "This is a shitty time to call. What the hell do you want?"

"I told you. Just checking that you made it back. Are you working on what we discussed?"

Justin cursed under his breath and felt a constriction in his throat. "Look, the past two days have been very busy. You pulled me away at a bad time, and I've been playing catch-up."

"That's really a shame, Jus, but my contacts had me call to let you know they are serious about the money."

"I'm sure they are," Justin became pale. "But I really haven't had time to give the matter much attention. Maybe by Monday I can get back to you. You didn't give me a contact number. Give me one now."

"You don't sound as if you fully understand, friend. This is not something that allows a lot of wait time. I tried to warn you what these people are like."

"Peter, I told you the situation. I'll work on the matter this weekend and get back to you. Give me your number." Justin was pissed and frightened at the same time. He sat thinking about the call and the events that preceded it for several minutes after putting down the phone. He got up and paced the room. He felt stuffy and closed in. He went upstairs, dressed and went outside. The crisp fall night cleared his head, and he felt calmer.

The sky was bright with stars. He realized he seldom noticed the night sky. "Does this say something about me," he whispered.

Justin walked slowly around the yard talking quietly aloud. "It doesn't seem possible that the groups Peter and Karl were connected to in Berlin can still be operating. Maybe there are two or three members still around. That's possible. More than ten years. Look what's happened in that time: a unified Germany, open borders throughout Europe, drug routes from Afghanistan, Albania and former Soviet republics." Justin walked into the driveway and the motion activated lights flashed on blinding him. "Shit!"

Back in the side yard, Justin's thoughts took a different path. "Karl. It must be Karl. He knows enough about what happened to sell the idea to some local group. He doesn't have to be trafficking to know how to make contact. Karl's street smart. And Peter. It wouldn't have been that hard to find out where Peter went when he left prison. He probably jumped at the opportunity when he was invited into the deal. Good old rich American Justin. Let's take him." Justin kicked at a toy left in the grass by his daughter. He raged on quietly, glad no one was hearing his tirade, talking to himself.

"And if I pay, what will keep them from coming back for more? Do they think I can be pressured by tying me to drug running in Berlin in the eighties? Fuck 'um. Threaten me? From Dresden and Toronto. No!"

Justin heard the soft sound from the tires of a passing car. Some people out late. The glow from the streetlights reached a corner of the yard. The rest was in darkness. Justin sat in a patio chair near the rose bushes, thinking, now silent.

What about the mention of Frankfurt?" Justin wrapped his arms against his chest feeling chilled. *A guess. Maybe Klaus is still working for the Army and dealing on the side. Karl's contacts can have connections in Frankfurt and have heard some story. Far-fetched, but possible. I bet it was a guess though. It's a way to accuse me of cashing in."*

Justin sighed. He was cold. He moved to the patio door. Quietly moving into the house he was reaching a conclusion. *What if Karl and Peter are playing this on their own? It doesn't explain how they're financing the meetings, but I don't know they don't have the resources. But either way, they can suck me dry if I make a payment. This situation must end. I'll call Peter tomorrow.*

* * *

The icy storm had become a heavy downpour and the afternoon light through the windows cast the room in deep shadows. Jackie got up to turn on some lights. "Justin never got to Dresden when he worked in Germany," she said returning to her chair. Alexis hoped she finally was going to get information she could use. She was tired and emotionally spent. "It was in the East and impossible for him to get clearance to visit. He was eager to work it into our trip, and we drove up from Prague. We stayed at the Kempinski Hotel, a rebuilt palace. Are you familiar with Dresden's history? We stayed three nights and had a wonderful time."

Jackie's enthusiasm for the visit began to fade as she continued. "However, late in the afternoon of our last day when we were picking up our key, the clerk told Justin that he had a visitor in the solarium." She clasped her hands tightly, rubbing them as though they were cold. "He was surprised and puzzled since he didn't know anyone in the city, and couldn't imagine who would be waiting. He told me it was probably a mistake, and sent me on up while he checked.

"About thirty minutes later, Jus came up. He was pale and shaken. Yet he tried to act calm and casual. He laughed and told me that an acquaintance named Karl, whom he had known years ago in Berlin, had seen us in the Zwinger Gardens the day before." Jackie paused as if realizing for the first time the strangeness of Karl's behavior. "His friend followed us to the hotel and found that sure enough, it was Justin. He said they chatted over a wine and—and that was that."

Alexis raised her eyebrows quizzically, "You didn't discuss the meeting again?"

"We had tickets for a concert having dinner in the hotel first, and Jus said we should start getting ready. He hugged me and tried to make it seem like nothing, but I could tell he was worried. I didn't try to push him to tell me more."

At this point, Alexis called time-out. "Jackie, this is all very intense for you, and more than a little confusing for me. I'm already thinking of happy hour. The weather's getting worse. I'd like to get my stuff from the car and make a phone call home to see that everything is going okay. Will that work?"

Jackie laughed for the first time that afternoon. "Of course. I'm sorry. Your room is all ready. I wasn't thinking. It's been . . ."

"No problem."

"Bring your things in and make the call from your room. Our nanny can get on the way home early before the weather gets worse. I'll pull out some spaghetti sauce from the freezer. There's plenty for salad and lots of vino on hand. Will that be okay for dinner? Paul and Laura will like having a guest."

"It sounds perfect. I'm anxious to meet your kids. I haven't seen them for two years and know they've grown as much as mine. We can talk more later or just kick back tonight and pick it up again tomorrow. I need some time to mull over what you've told me so far."

Jackie sounded relieved. "And we're good for happy hour as well! I really appreciate you coming. I probably should have called sooner, but I kept waiting for Jus to contact me. I couldn't believe he would disappear without a word. I just haven't known where to turn. To be honest, Phillip isn't a bit of help. He keeps telling me we should be doing more, and when I ask what, he doesn't know. But he is doing a good job of taking charge at the office. Justin would be very pleased.

* * *

November: McLean, Virginia

In spite of the fractured night, Justin rose early. He was in a sour mood and wouldn't discuss the late call with Jackie. He told her he had to go to the office to finish something he had left undone the day before. Later, Justin called Peter. Following a long delay, Peter came to the phone.

"Look, Peter," Justin began. "I've been thinking the whole thing through, and it adds up to you and Karl running the deal to squeeze me for money." He decided to be aggressively direct.

Peter laughed, "That's crazy. Do you really think that? Come on Justin. Don't be a fool."

"Whether you are or not, it's not possible for me to come up with the money. You and Karl have an exaggerated idea of how much I'm worth. I can't possibly put together that kind of cash. My bank account doesn't have anything near the amount."

"You're a real fool, Jus. Just like always. I'll pass your message along. Someone else will contact you." The line went dead.

Justin sat at his desk and wiped his hands, which were wet with perspiration. He looked out a window and saw only a bare parking lot with a small grass area and a fountain beyond. The fountain was off for the winter. He got up and paced the room. It was tastefully furnished, although not extravagant. He believed it reflected the kind of person he was.

Justin once more considered the situation. *What kind of connection can they have here in the U.S.? Whoever they are, it should be clear that I couldn't and wouldn't agree to the demands.* He put on his coat and left his office to go home. *At least I've got a reprieve for now. We'll see what Louis thinks about it tomorrow.*

Chapter Three

Saturday afternoon, Alexis flew home still trying to make sense out of Jackie's story. She remained unconvinced there was a sinister explanation for Justin's disappearance, although some evidence pointed in that direction. Alexis understood why Jackie might think there was a connection between the unexpected meeting with Karl and the unexpected appearance of Peter, but found no justification for connecting the two with the accident on the Parkway. Had Justin and Jackie really been followed and attacked, or was it a drunken hit and run as the police believed? Jackie's an intelligent woman, Alexis told herself, but she sometimes exaggerates. Could Jackie be suppressing a fear that Justin had abandoned her?

Sunday, Alexis relaxed with the children. Monday, after seeing Luke and Becky off to school she rang up Travis. It took several rings until his groggy voice answered. "Yeah."

"Travis? Time to rally! I brought some work for you."

"Huh? Oh. Alexis. What time is it? I didn't get to bed until two or so."

"Five," she said to tease him. "Well, eight at least. Is someone with you?"

"No."

"Then work your way over. I'll fix you breakfast."

Travis was Alexis' part time assistant. Alexis let him live in the apartment over the garage in her large Southern Shores home as partial salary. It was a good arrangement for both, and her kids loved him. So did Leonidas, an approval Alexis viewed as a good character reference.

Alexis discovered Travis a few months after her husband's death one late afternoon at Keoni's Wave, a local hangout for surfers overlooking the Kill

Devil Hill beach. A friend who owned the restaurant told her Travis was a computer whiz who dropped out of Rose-Hulman Institute in his sophomore year and joined the Navy to become a SEAL. At the time, this seemed a strange choice to those who knew the green and purple haired youth at home and the college, but Travis surprised them all. Then, he told his friends, a few years after serving in the Gulf War, he burned out. Finishing his last tour, he sought an unfettered life with emphasis on riding the waves. For extra money he tended bar when he wasn't working with one of the dive schools in the area.

"What's up?" Travis demanded, entering the kitchen. He made no attempt to look bright and alert.

"Grab some coffee while I fix your eggs. We'll talk while you eat." Travis filled a cup and dropped into a chair. Sun poured through the kitchen window. Music from a local beach station played quietly in the background while Alexis cooked eggs and dished up the rest of the sausage she had fixed for Luke and Becky. They preferred cereal, but from time to time they agreed to eat something else.

While Travis ate, Alexis busied herself by rinsing off some dishes and stacking them in the dishwasher. Checking that Travis was pretty well awake and ready, Alexis began. "What we have is a missing husband, Justin Lawrence, father of two, second marriage, successful and financially secure, as in rich. The wife says they're happy, adore their children, and have an active social life. Justin has extensive investments and owns major interest in a car dealership in the D.C. metro area. Investments are handled in New York where, by the way, he grew up. Brooklyn." Alexis reached for a file as she continued.

"Starting in mid-October, he's had pressure and threats from some person or persons his wife has never met. Justin told her things were under control, but while supposedly on a hunting trip with long time buddies from New York he disappeared. Except it turns out there was no hunting trip."

Travis looked up with growing interest. Alexis spread a stack of papers across the large table: copies of the Lawrence bank statements, investment reports, and various phone and fax numbers at home and work, as well as credit card numbers. "Justin's 4x4 SUV is also missing, and to date there is no trace. When Jackie first tried to report her husband missing, she was told it was too soon. Once authorities accepted the report, the Virginia police put out an APB. They particularly enlisted the help of the New York State and City police since that was Justin's destination. Not a sign of him. Jackie told me the last time she talked with Jus was the afternoon he arrived in Armonk where he was joining his friends. Since the friends didn't actually meet, it's possible the call was made from someplace else." She stopped at this point to give Travis a chance to comment.

"What do you think?" Travis asked as he sopped up his eggs with toast.
"I'm still thinking. What's your first impression?"

Travis finished the eggs and gulped his coffee. "It sounds like her man is dumping her, or else they're running some sort of a scam. Did she tell the police about the strange events? Do we know much more?"

Alexis told him Jackie's story about Dresden and that Justin knew Peter and Karl when he worked in Berlin. "Could what's happened be connected to Berlin?" she asked.

Travis paused, "Let me think." He handed Alexis his mug motioning for a refill. She reached over to the counter for the pot and topped if off. "This old Cold War thing is a stretch," Travis said slowly. "It's possible, but I have trouble buying it. What about his business interests and social life? Does he gamble?"

* * *

September: Dresden, Germany

Justin was led to a table in the Solarium of the Kimpinski Hotel, and after a short take was stunned to recognize his visitor. "Karl, what a surprise! It's been years," he said in German to the former DDR colonel waiting for him. As they exchanged greetings, Justin's surprise was replaced by a surge of alarm. *How did he know I was here? Why does he want to meet?*

"I thought I recognized you yesterday crossing the Zwinger Gardens and followed you and the woman to the hotel to be sure. Yes, it is a surprise. I never thought I would see you again after all the years that have passed." While Karl spoke, Justin looked closely at the man across the table. He had aged: close cropped gray hair, gaunt face, and formless worn suit. Conditions had been hard, Justin supposed. At the same time, the man's eyes were alert with the same penetrating look that Justin remembered from the checkpoint crossing.

"*Weiss wein, bitte.*" Justin said to the waiter. "*Ein Halb Karaffe.*"

Once the wine was served, Karl revealed the purpose of his visit. Karl, once the conductor, now Karl, the messenger.

"I was in touch last night with some old contacts to tell them you were in Dresden. They got back to me this morning just before lunch. They told me to meet with you and let you know you'll be hearing from them." Seated at ease, Karl smiled politely over his glass of wine, a smile not reflected in his eyes. "I wasn't sure it would be possible, but here we are."

"Why would your old contacts want to be in touch with me?" Justin felt himself stiffen and glared at Karl. *This can't be happening. I put it all behind me years ago.*

At the time, I was foolish. Really stupid. But I got away with it all. I've got a new life now.

"They didn't tell me much, but I believe they think you owe them something for undelivered goods. It's not anything I've thought about for a long time, but others, it seems, have longer memories." Karl looked closely at Justin as though trying to read his reaction. "It's about that last transport you made. When our colleague was arrested."

"That's crazy!" Justin realized he was showing alarm. He didn't want Karl to know he was frightened. He took a deep breath and spoke more evenly. "All that was settled before I left Berlin. One group or the other took the shipment and trashed my car in the process. I never got my fee for transporting it either." Jus sipped his wine. He could feel himself begin to perspire under his shirt. He wondered if Karl could tell.

"So I've heard. There does seem to have been some confusion back then; even I felt the pressure." Karl topped off his glass from the karaffe. "At the time, someone contacted me and asked about you crossing. I told them everything had gone as before. Then I was able to transfer out, and they left me alone." Karl chuckled, but to Justin his eyes were dark and menacing. "Now it seems they think differently. Wasn't it fortunate you came to Dresden after all these years, and I was here to recognize you?"

* * *

On the Outer Banks, Alexis and Travis continued their discussion, looking over bank statements as well as credit card and phone bills provided by Jackie. Alexis cleared away remaining dishes from the table and put them in the sink. She returned to the table and again picked up the conversation. "Jackie said the police believed that the accident on the Parkway was caused by a reckless or drunken driver and Justin didn't contest it, although she thinks from his actions at the time that he had other suspicions. That's why she didn't think they would take her seriously if she tried to connect Justin's disappearance to the hit and run. So she told them he hasn't come home, and that the friends didn't go hunting."

"No wonder they weren't too quick to take it up."

"That's where we are so far." Alexis genuinely liked Travis and thought highly of him. She knew he could be a serious player, but to get anywhere she had to play to his laid back demeanor by using his language and not sounding too self important. "That's why I'm putting you to work. Jackie's given me the documents I asked for as starters. Justin's dropped out of sight, but there is no hard evidence pointing to foul play. She gave me a hefty retainer and says she wants to find him. I told her I have to think about it some more." Alexis waited a moment before concluding. "I'm still not sure I want to get deeply involved. So for now, I want you to use your wizardry with the computer and see if anything turns up in these accounts that give any clues." Alexis pushed back from the table waving her hand at the documents scattered in piles.

Travis picked up a phone bill and looked at it more closely. "Why are you undecided? Do you think Jackie is being honest with you?"

Alexis didn't answer right away. She got up and walked over to a window looking out at the bright sea to collect her thoughts. "I'm not sure. It's a complicated situation, but I somehow feel that Lucas would expect me to help. He introduced Jackie to Justin when we were all skiing in the Dolomites. She's the sister of Lucas' best friend who was assigned to Naples at the same time we were there."

Travis took a long look at Alexis. She didn't often speak of Lucas, so he knew it was sensitive ground. "Do I think you're dropping place names again?"

Alexis started and turned away from the window. "I didn't mean to. It's just that I don't feel I can turn Jackie down because the story sounds a little thin or crazy. She insisted I take a retainer, although she knows I don't really need it. But I think she asked me because she wants to keep the inquiry private. Her lawyer has pressed her not to get any investigators involved, although she's not sure why, and she has told friends outside the family that Justin's away on business."

Another silence filled the air except for the low music and banter in the background. Alexis lapsed once more in thought. Jackie had been studying in Florence when she joined them skiing in Italy. She and her brother Chris were close, and he was very much the protective big brother. Justin appeared on the scene to ski with his teenage sons, Matthias and Philip, whom he brought out of the West Berlin enclave within East Germany. Justin never brought his wife, Anna, which Alexis always thought unusual. Justin flirted openly with women, single and attached, on the slopes and in discos, which included Jackie that Christmas vacation.

Travis looked into his cup waiting for Alexis to continue. "So yes," Alexis came back to the present, "there might be something going on between Justin and her that she didn't divulge. His past behavior doesn't exactly inspire confidence. But for now, we play it that he's disappeared, and she doesn't know what to do."

Without giving Travis a chance for reply, Alexis went on. "We need to know about those phone calls from Peter, and if Justin might have made any to him. Also, we want to look for any significant sales or movement of assets from Justin's accounts with his bank and broker. Find out where Justin stayed on his trips to New York. See if he actually stayed somewhere near Armonk, if you can. I think for now you make a quiet review of

Justin's affairs and contacts while I look a little more into what Jackie has told me, and Justin's recent activities. I'll call New York to talk with those guys Justin claimed he was hunting with when he disappeared."

"I'll get on it. But has Jackie told us everything?"

"Like I said," Alexis cleared the cups from the table, "I haven't decided what I think. It sounds like something out of a LeCarre novel, but who knows these days? Before the Wall came down, most people seldom thought about what went on in Germany, but now they don't think about it at all. Americans have a short attention span for what goes on too far outside of town."

Travis gave her an appraising look. "Come down from the soap box," he said with a laugh. "I'll get to work on this stuff."

After Travis left, Alexis took her coffee out on the deck. It was sunny and crisp. Pulling another jacket around her hooded sweatshirt, she took a sheltered spot in the sun out of the wind and gazed thoughtfully out at the ocean. *What would Lucas think of this? It seems so improbable.* She let herself drift. Lucas. Lucas. So intuitive. So insightful. How she still missed him.

The ocean beyond the dunes sparkled from the sunlight. Alexis could hear the surf hitting the beach. It was a view she and Lucas often shared together in close silence.

After he left the Navy, Lucas and she worked together with his private agency. They also started a security system company in Kitty Hawk on the Outer Banks, protecting houses and businesses in Duck, Corolla and south towards Hatteras. He tutored her in both businesses, but she didn't think she had his insight. Yet, several months after his death she accepted an assignment to track down the heir to a property in Nags Head. Her success gave her confidence, and other jobs followed. She was gratified clients were giving her their vote for competency. Alexis shifted in her seat following with her gaze some birds lazily skimming the waves. She continued to think about Lucas.

He had died in a skiing accident in Aspen. An excellent skier and a risk taker, he skied away from the group off *piste* and somehow fell at an unexpected drop. At least that's what the ski patrol reported. It was never clear. Just that he died. Alexis still struggled to understand. The accident also had added to her discomfort with Justin. He was nearby when Lucas skied away, and he was the one who brought back the news to Alexis at the condo.

Now two years later, she wondered what her husband would think of this situation with Justin. Lucas once confided that Jus left Berlin under a cloud, a statement on which he never expanded. On several occasions

Lucas had been sent to Berlin by Naval Intelligence, and Alexis believed that was how he knew about Justin's activities. Although the couples socialized in McLean and Aspen, Lucas always seemed a bit distrustful of Justin and quietly guarded in their relationship. How she wished they could discuss the situation now.

Finally, taking the last sip of coffee, Alexis decided this wasn't getting her anywhere. She told Jackie she would do some preliminary examination of the situation before deciding whether or not to take the case, and it was time to get started. Alexis went back inside leaving the sound of the surf to the gulls.

* * *

November: McLean, Virginia

It was noon when Justin woke. He was groggy, and the pain immediate when he moved. It all rushed back: the crash, the police, the ambulance, the emergency room, Jackie. *Where is Jackie?* He groaned as he sat up.

Philip had come for him at the hospital late in the night. Cathy, Phillip's wife, had stayed with him and the children. The doctors said nothing was broken. They told him to see his own doctor for a follow-up evaluation. They kept Jackie for observation. Jackie! Justin put his head in his hands. *"The bastards!"*

The rest of the day, Justin lay in bed thinking, slipping back and forth between medicated sleep and awake. He was stunned by how much he and his family were threatened. He was in a box.

Over the next few days, Justin fluctuated from one decision to another. Frightened by the attack, he convinced himself he had to turn over some money. He would tell Peter that one hundred thousand was all he could scrape together. They would have to be satisfied. After talking it over with Louis, he went back to his original thought that they probably would keep pressing him. Justin vacillated; other ideas filtered in his thoughts. He began searching the web.

On a cold gray day, the phone rang at Justin's desk. He picked it up, "Justin Lawrence."

The voice was accented but smooth. "I'm a friend of Peter. I'm calling to check your progress on getting together the payment."

Justin went rigid, his hand gripped the phone. *My God. Calling me here in my office! In the middle of the day! I can't believe it.* "Who did you say you are? I didn't quite catch your name." Justin tried to sound calm.

"I didn't give you a name. I'm Peter's connection. We want to know how soon you're going to have the first payment." Justin judged the man's tone as polite but menacing.

Justin thought quickly and turned in his chair to look out at the threatening weather. "The truth is I've been recovering from injuries I suffered in an accident, and haven't had the time or energy to deal with much else." He had been expecting something, but not here at the office.

"That's interesting, Mr. Lawrence, but now that you're better it's time to get the first delivery together. We're watching you." The caller hung up.

Shaken, but still undecided, Justin began the process of putting together five hundred thousand dollars in cash. He hated the idea of facing the scene at his bank and the unasked questions in everyone's eyes. Packing a case with cash and walking out. He continued to simmer in resentment at the situation and met again with Louis.

Chapter Four

With Christmas approaching, few work orders required attention at the security systems office in Kitty Hawk, and Alexis busied herself preparing the house for the holidays. The days were gray, and blustery winds whipped the area. At the back of her mind she continued to puzzle over Justin's disappearance, and waited with mixed feelings for Travis to report. He had been working for three days, glued almost non-stop to the computers. Using account numbers and passwords provided by Jackie, he gained access into the Lawrence bank accounts, investment transactions, and credit card purchases.

A little after three on the third day, Travis phoned over from the office to Alexis working in the house. "I've compiled some interesting information. Do you want to come over now or wait until the morning?"

"I'll be right over. Do you have anything that tells us what has happened to Justin?" Alexis reached for a sweater from the back of a chair and prepared to cross the walkway to the small office adjacent to the apartment over the extended double garage.

"Not yet, but there's been some unusual movement of money between several accounts. And a couple of other things of interest. I'll show you when you get here." Travis hunched his shoulders to loosen the tightness from long hours of sitting. He was eager for a long run in the cold air and waited impatiently to make his report.

A small table in the middle of the room was littered with piles of printed material and the records brought from McLean. The trash basket was full of discarded Styrofoam food trays and cups, evidence that Travis had taken few breaks from his computer while searching for information about Justin Lawrence and his activities.

Travis was in a side alcove with the computers when Alexis opened the door, but he called to her when he heard her enter. "I'll be right there. Just finishing one last printout."

Alexis cleared away takeout debris from the desk at a window overlooking the dunes which surrounded the house. She sat down turning the chair towards the table waiting for Travis to start his report. The room was hot and she took off the sweater. "Do you have anything that will help make up my mind to go forward with the case? I've got to get back to Jackie sometime soon."

"That will be for you to decide." Travis came into the larger room with several pages of printed material in his hand. "But either way, I'd like to go to D.C. and sit down at the computers in Justin's home and at his office. I'd like to check if there's some software and records accessible that may give us some more clues. I have some contacts up there that may be helpful. Do we know who their attorney is? Is he up there also? Do we have any phone numbers for him?" Speaking in a rush, Travis grabbed a bottle of water from a shelf over the small refrigerator and sat down at the table.

It took a few seconds for Alexis to absorb all the ideas Travis had launched at her. "Whoa. It's almost Christmas. I'm not sure Jackie will be eager for such an intrusion just now. Can we wait?"

"We can, but the longer we do, the colder the trail becomes. I wouldn't bother her, just sit down in Justin's study and play with his computer setup. Also the one he uses at work. Maybe explore the business network." Travis drank deeply from the bottle.

Alexis frowned and shook her head. "From what I've heard and seen so far, I didn't think I'd be able to do much more about the case until after New Year's. If I ask that you come up, she'll think I'm going to take it on for sure. I just don't know that I will."

Travis stood up and began to pace the room. "She and the kids won't even know I'm there other than to answer a few questions. And at the office? Who's in charge while Justin's away, the son Philip?"

Sensing that Travis was agitated by her reluctance to readily agree to the trip, Alexis moved her chair closer to the table. "Philip's been working closely with his father since Justin's uncle sold him major interest in the business. The uncle has retired to Florida and the Caribbean with his millions. I don't know Phillip's position in the office. There are other more senior execs."

Alexis paused before arguing. "But I'm expecting the kids' grandfather, Captain, at the end of the week to spend Christmas with us, and I'm also getting the clothes and ski equipment out for the week after with my folks and Sam's family in Aspen. It's the first time we've gone since Lucas' accident, and I'm a little tense about it. Besides, don't you have plans to go up to your sister's in New Jersey?" Determined to get on with the report, Alexis leaned over to pick up one of the printouts on the table.

"But Christmas isn't until the middle of next week, and I can get a little look before then. Nobody's paying much attention to anything, and I won't be noticed. It's a good time, and I have some leads and questions that we can go after before too much time goes by. You think I can have access at his office during the weekend? Promise to be low profile. Is Captain staying over while you're off?"

Alexis looked over the paper and replied to the last question. "Yes, he'll be here looking after the dogs and sit the house until we get back after the New Year. It was his vacation home at one time. He loves it here. He'll also look at the boat. It has been out of the water for a couple years over in Wanchese. You two can share war stories when you get back. Take him down to Keoni's maybe." she looked up and smiled as she envisioned the retired naval captain in the clutches of carefree, irreverent surfers.

Noting Alexis' desire to hear what he'd found so far, Travis pulled closer to the table and picked up the report. "Sounds okay to me. By the way, Justin stayed at the Ramada in Armonk the night he drove up from D.C. for his so-called hunting trip!" Travis offered the information he thought was the most important he had found.

"Confirmed?" Alexis looked up surprised.

"I found it on his VISA account. Last charge made so far that's shown up." Maybe the information would help push her to agree to his trip to D.C.

"Only one night?"

"No, two. Wednesday and Thursday."

"That is of interest. Ron, Justin's friend in Armonk, told Jackie he hadn't seen Jus. I need to call him for a chat to see if he tells the same story. What else do you have here," Alexis pointed to the papers. "I'll decide whether to call up to Jackie to ask if you may come."

* * *

November: Arlington, Virginia

Although Justin discreetly met with an official at his bank to arrange the cash transfer, he was unable to face the scene of picking it up where he was known. So the withdrawal took place from an Arlington branch in Crystal City. Justin met the bank manager in his office where he was treated with respect and without questions.

"Mr. Lawrence, Ms Hue will accompany you to the vault level. She will remain with you to count out the cash withdrawal you arranged," the manager instructed politely.

"Thank you, Mr. Llewellyn. That will be fine. I brought a bag which I believe will accommodate everything. My driver is waiting." The last statement was a lie. Justin was humiliated. *What are they thinking about him?*

Ms Hue led Justin to an elevator, inserted a control key for the door, and motioned him inside. They traveled down two flights into the basement of the bank and entered an anteroom to the vault.

"The order is ready on the table in the recess on the right. Mr. Owens here will assist in the count." She introduced a man waiting at a small desk. Justin entered the room pulling the bag behind.

Later, flushed with anger and embarrassment, Justin pushed through the door of the bank and stepped into the bright sun slanting through the tall buildings. For a moment he was blinded, and across the street against the glare he discerned a black silhouetted figure. Startled, for an instance, he imagined himself walking down the steps of the East German checkpoint building as Karl watched from across the parking lot. Justin blinked and looked away from the sun. He started to perspire and his scalp prickled. *No, not Karl. I must be losing it. But who is that? Did they follow me from the parking garage?*

Justin breathed deeply to compose himself. "Damn!" he said under his breath. The man across the street crossed at the light and continued on his way. *It's nobody I know. Nobody followed me when I left the car. I'm sure of it.*

The bag Justin had carried to the bank for the cash was a suitcase with wheels and a collapsible handle. Although the parking garage was only a short distance, Justin worried about pulling the bag from the bank back to the van. He felt conspicuous and vulnerable. He felt like a fool wheeling five hundred thousand dollars through the streets of Crystal City.

Justin looked around and walked two blocks to the garage. Images of the walks from the garage near Louise's flat in East Berlin, and the feeling that he was being watched flashed through his thoughts.

After a few minutes Justin reached the 4X4: the van with the tracking device discovered by his mechanic attached underneath. He threw the heavy bag into the back and headed to the pay booth.

Anger replaced the fear Justin had felt. Tonight, he would load the van. Tomorrow, on the way out of town, he would drop by the shop and, tipping well, have Danny remove the device and place it on another car.

Justin closed his eyes. He felt the start of a headache. Before pulling out of the parking lot, he reached in his coat pocket, stretched his hand across his chest, and pulled his trigger finger. He gripped the steering wheel hard and drove off.

* * *

Travis leaned back in his chair, his feet stretched out up on the table. He talked while Alexis scanned the printouts. "The stuff about his bank drafts and on-line checking you can look over later. I didn't see anything special that caught my eye. The movement of a large sum of money is what you should look at now. Go to about page three." Travis waited for Alexis to find the section before he continued.

"Most of Justin's capital assets are handled by a major investment banking firm in New York. His portfolio also contains a substantial money market account, available for withdrawals. During the first week in November, five hundred thousand dollars were deposited into the money account. I haven't been able to determine the source. It came from out of the country. Possibly a bank in Luxembourg or Lichtenstein. I'll look into this later. That's one reason I want to look at Justin's computer files, software, and business accounts." Alexis nodded, acknowledging she now understood his desire to go to McLean.

Travis shifted and drank some more water "Two days later, the same amount was transferred from the New York account to Justin's personal account in a Washington bank. In addition, he and Jackie shared a joint account, and Jackie has her own personal account with another Washington bank."

Alexis interrupted, "Probably the one connected to her Washingtonian family. Interesting, but it can be confusing. Go on." She put the report on the table and turned over pages face down as she finished with each.

The day before Justin left for New York, the five hundred thou was withdrawn from a branch in Crystal City. I want to find out what happened to this money, if possible. So far there is no record it was re-deposited. Justin is somewhere carrying a chunk of cash." Travis got up and stretched. Alexis quickly scanned the last pages. "So do you think I can go to D.C.?" he asked. "All the raw data is stored in a computer file if you want to look it over on your own."

Alexis made up her mind. "You're sure you want to go up this week?" With a nod from Travis, Alexis reached for the phone and called Jackie to see what she could arrange.

Later in the afternoon, Alexis called Ron's home and got his wife, Martha, who said Ron usually was home by six or so. She asked that Alexis call after dinner. Martha also offered Alexis his office number in the City.

Martha said she hadn't seen Justin for over a year. "I'm really sorry to hear of his disappearance. I know Jackie's distressed. I remember her call in November. I don't know what to think. It's very unlike Justin. Ron's known him since they were school pals, and we visited him in Germany several times when he was married to Anna."

Martha kept talking without waiting for comment from Alexis. "From what I could tell, he and Jackie have been very happy since they've been together. I can only guess that something dreadful has happened to him. He's always been something of a lady's man, I'd say, but underneath not irresponsible. Just disappearing isn't his style."

Alexis let Martha come up for air, and ended the conversation. "I appreciate your talking with me. Please let Ron know I'll be calling. Thanks again." Alexis hung up and thought about the brief conversation.

Martha had touched on one of the issues that continued to nag at her conscience, Justin and his flirtatious behavior. Could he be off on another romantic pursuit?

Alexis thought back to the subtle advances Justin made when she first met him that winter skiing with Lucas. The next year he pursued Jackie, although she wasn't with a husband. And Jus flirted openly with the girl friend or wife of an Italian man in Cortina at a local disco. The man almost knocked Justin's head off. Sometimes this behavior went on in front of his sons. What had Anna thought of Justin's roving eye, and how had it played in their relationship? So far, all Alexis had was Jackie's version of Justin's encounters and phone calls. Could his trip to New York in October have been a tryst of some sort? She shook her head to clear her thoughts. *Let's stay objective. There are several possibilities.*

Alexis decided she needed to go out for awhile. She put on her jacket and left to check with her office manager at the security office in Kitty Hawk and do some shopping: groceries, Christmas gifts, the cleaners. The air was chilly and a brisk wind blew from the north. December wasn't the best month to be out on the Banks.

By the time Alexis called Ron that evening, she had talked with Martin Gavin, the other hunting pal. The reason the three men did not make their annual trip, Martin told her, was because he traveled to London for a conference and remained a few days with his wife through Thanksgiving. "We were gone a little over two weeks, almost three. Ron, Jus, and I couldn't work out another time, although I told them to go ahead and use the camp. They weren't up for that, and neither of their wives wanted to go with them. Maybe in the spring or summer sometime, they said. So we decided to skip it altogether. First time in six years."

"Did Jus talk with you any other time before you left? Perhaps in mid October when Jackie said he went to New York?"

"He was here in October? No, he didn't get in touch, although I can't say he calls every trip. I know he and Jackie went to Europe in September, but after they got back our only contact was about the hunting trip when I made plans around the conference."

"Is there a key to the cabin that's easily accessible?"

"It's kept locked, but someone could break in. Ron, up in Armonk, has a key, and there's a caretaker I pay a little to look in once in awhile. He has one too, but he doesn't give it out unless he confirms it with me. Do you think Jus used the camp after all?"

"I have no reason to think so. I'm just looking into all the possibilities. You've been very helpful, Mr. Gavin. Do you mind if I call again if I think of something?"

"Not at all. I want to help. And please call me Martin. Do you think I should check with Henry to see if anyone's been up there?"

"If you do, that would be fine."

"I'll call if I think of or hear something."

As she hung up the phone, Alexis was impressed and gratified by how eager Martin was to help solve the mystery of his friend. His warm bond with Justin was evident. He, like Ron, had grown up with Justin. Justin once told Alexis in a casual conversation that he, Ron, and Martin were the triumvirate of their Brooklyn neighborhood, although some of the more reserved used the word terror. Alexis believed it was a kinder time.

After Martin's eagerness to help, talking with Ron was another story. "Yes, this is Ron Creighton. I have a few minutes to spare you, Mrs. Mason, but there's nothing much I can offer to explain where my buddy is. Martha told me of your call, and she checked with Jackie about you. Are you a well-known agent? Where did I hear you work out of?"

"I appreciate you giving me some time, Mr. Creighton," Alexis ignored the condescending tone. "I talked with Martin Gavin earlier, and he was very concerned. He said he was out of the country when Justin disappeared, but was sure you wouldn't hesitate to do what you could to help."

"You spoke with Martin?"

At the first hostile vibes, Alexis decided to proceed with caution. She wasn't sure why Ron was so defensive, but she knew he had told Jackie he didn't see her husband, even though Alexis knew two nights in Armonk appeared on Justin's VISA. "Yes. He said the conference in London was the reason the three of you didn't go on your hunting trip, and that you and Jus didn't want to go without him."

"That's right." Ron concurred. "We decided it just wouldn't be the same, and our wives weren't interested. Jus wants to bring his son once he's a little older, but thought this year he was still too young."

"Can you think of any reason why Jus would come up other than to hunt? Jackie says he called her the evening he arrived in Armonk, and told her that the two of you would be off the next day."

The phone was silent a moment. "I didn't know he hadn't told Jackie. Jus knew early in October we weren't making the trip. He said Jackie wasn't interested in the cold woods in November." Another silence. Alexis waited him out. "Then again, maybe he had somebody he wanted to spend the weekend with." Alexis looked more attentive and arched her brow at what Ron was suggesting. She thought of her earlier speculations after the conversation with Martha.

"And run off with? Could he have had something that special going on Jackie wouldn't suspect?" Alexis pressed aggressively.

"I don't know." Ron had grown more reticent. "It doesn't seem that he would do that. How long has it been now, five or six weeks?"

"That's right, Mr. Creighton. Almost six weeks. No trace. No contact." More silence. Alexis could hear the TV from the room down the hall where her kids were watching. *Too loud.*

"Look, call me Ron." His tone had altered to sound more concerned and puzzled. "You know, Jus and I grew up together. We've been pals forever. He's probably my best friend along with Martin. I don't know what to think." There was a long pause. "As you know, Justin always had a reckless streak. Once his father turned around the family department store after the war, there was lots of money. Some of us thought he got a bit out of control. All he seemed interested in was being a frat playboy and making big money himself some day." Ron unleashed a dam of thoughts long held back. "Then he flunked out of Cornell and joined the army. I mean, I wasn't exactly a grind, but I had sense enough to graduate."

Ron hesitated, reflecting on what he'd had said, and continued, "We met up again when I was in the Air Force in Germany, and all went back to normal with us. Jus was discharged in Europe without coming back to the States, and went right to work for the Exchange Services. He didn't want to face his father. He was a natural manager though. He got along with the brass and had good ideas, so he advanced quickly."

"Ron, please call me Alexis. I agree with you. We don't have to be so formal. I think we're both on the same side.

"Let me ask you, would it help any if you know we've confirmed that Justin stayed there at the Ramada for two nights, and his call to Jackie definitely came from Armonk the evening he arrived?" Another long silence on the other end caused Alexis to wonder if they had been disconnected.

In Armonk, Ron struggled with his emotions. He felt his eyes welling with tears. *Two nights? He stayed here? He said he was going back to the City. Jus, what's happened to you? Where are you, buddy?* Ron looked around his den sanctuary. There was a fireplace with two comfortable chairs in front, his desk, a half wall of books and trophies, some prints. On one wall was a locked gun cabinet containing his rifles. He took a deep breath. "Look," he said to Alexis, "could you hold a minute?"

Ron got up from the desk, and went to the mini bar. He poured a stiff shot of whiskey and took a sip. He looked at the photo of him with Jus and Martin in full hunting regalia posed with a buck at their feet. He silently toasted the two and returned to the phone.

"Mrs. Mason, Alexis," he spoke hesitantly. "Look," he took a big breath, "I did see Jus that Wednesday evening. He called me at the office and asked to meet him at a place down the road for a drink before I went home. He said it was important that Martha not know. Now that you tell me he told Jackie we were going hunting, I can guess why." Another pause. Alexis could hear the hum in the line.

"It turned out he wanted to have me keep his Purdey for awhile. It was pretty strange, I admit, but he said he was going back to the City that evening. He said if Jackie ever asked, to be sure to tell her I hadn't seen him."

Gripping the phone more tightly in anticipation, Alexis asked, "Did he say anything else about why he was in New York?"

"Not exactly. He let me think he was spending a long weekend with a lady friend, but didn't say so as such."

"Anything else?"

"Not too much. Look. I don't really feel comfortable talking about this over the phone. You know?" Ron looked toward the door to be sure Martha couldn't hear.

Alexis quickly took the invitation. "If I can get up tomorrow, will you meet with me to talk?"

"In town would be best. Yes, I'll meet. I can break away from work or take a long lunch. I really hate this. I was trying to do my buddy a favor."

"I'll start right now to see how soon I can get up there. I'll be leaving from Norfolk. I'll call you sometime in the morning at your office once I'm on my way."

"OK," Ron sighed. "It's a date." He hung up the phone and walked over to the window. He stared out into the cold December night finishing his drink and thinking about his friend.

Alexis immediately started making arrangements for a quick trip to New York. It would set her back in Christmas preparations, but Captain wasn't a problem, and her kids were flexible. Earlier, Travis had left for McLean.

Late that evening, thinking back over the conversation with Ron, Alexis felt a sense of dread. What she had heard so far wasn't sounding good. She turned off the lights in her office and stood, looking out the window toward the dark ocean. *His Purdey. What's a Purdey?*

Chapter Five

A crisp breeze buffeted the sand on the path over the dune as Alexis finished her run and entered the kitchen. Travis greeted her with a mug of coffee, and suggested they talk on the porch out of the wind. Grabbing a jacket, she walked out and curled down in a favorite chair. Leonidas flopped down next to her, still panting from his furious race up and down the beach.

"How did things go in Aspen?"

"Not bad." Alexis propped her feet on the porch rail. "Actually very well. It was hard at first being where Lucas died, but my father and mother took charge of the children and their ski lessons, and Sam and Jen took charge of me. By the second night we were having a great time. It was nice being together to welcome the new millennium. How about you?"

Travis hooked a leg over the arm of his chair. "Everything went fine. When I got back, I spent some time with the captain. We looked over the boat in Wancheese and tracked down a smaller one he will use to teach your kids."

"He told me about it on the phone. I think it's a great idea. We often went out with Lucas, and it's good they'll continue to learn from their grandfather. Captain never quite forgave Lucas for leaving the Academy, even though eventually he received a commission." Alexis looked out at the view of dunes and ocean she never grew tired of.

"Dad also wasn't sure he approved of Intelligence as a real job for a naval officer. The two didn't see much of each other for several years before Lucas died. Captain harbors deep regret, I believe, and he's eager to bond with the kids."

"He wouldn't go with me to Keoni's though." Travis smiled broadly thinking of Captain's refusal.

"No? I can't imagine." Alexis laughed. She actually felt a weight of some kind finally lifting with the way the family was coming together. All of them had enjoyed themselves in Aspen: she, her parents, Sam and Jen, the cousins, and her children. It had been good to get back to the snow and mountains. Memories of her California youth at Mammoth, where she spent so much time slussing the slopes and hiking the mountains, had been reawakened.

"Captain said you made a quick trip to New York just before he came. Did you find out anything useful?"

Alexis sat up and pulled her jacket tightly around her. "Yes and no. We're no closer to knowing what happened to Justin. He did meet with Ron, and asked him to hold on to a favorite rifle. He took it with him from McLean, presumably to keep up the appearance of going hunting. Justin told Ron he was going back into the City, and thought it would be safer in Armonk."

"That's pretty strange, isn't it? I mean, why not take a not-so-special one if he was going to leave it?" Travis sat up in his chair and looked at Alexis.

"Did you notice the collection of handguns in Justin's study? Small, but very select, mostly European. Several rifles, too."

"No, I didn't. I can't explain his behavior. It's just one more event that happened, which makes his disappearance so inexplicable. This affection for rifles and handguns is something I don't understand. Ron said that particular rifle was special to Jus. Some kind of prized sporting rifle he bought in London. Took it on all their trips to the camp, although he seldom used it."

"You don't understand because you're a girl," Travis remarked in a teasing tone.

Alexis ignored the comment. "Maybe Justin wanted his friend to have it in case something happened to him. More important is that he insinuated to Ron that he was meeting a woman in New York, and not to tell Jackie, if she asked, that Ron had seen him. Ron didn't say anything to Martha, and slipped the rifle into the rack along with his own."

Travis nodded. "Didn't Ron think meeting him and leaving the gun was odd?"

Alexis hugged her coffee mug in her hand, and propped her feet once more on the rail. "Ron said he didn't feel great about it, but he couldn't turn him down. They have been friends forever. If it weren't for the rifle, Jus wouldn't have confided in him."

"Did Jus say when he would come back for it?"

"Sooner or later, but he left it open ended."

"Sounds crazy. Did Ron think it would be more than a long weekend?" Travis stood to pet Leonidas, and leaned back against the house.

"Not at the time. When the disappearance dragged on, Ron said he tried to put it out of his thoughts. Apparently Jus has always strayed a bit from one woman to another, but Ron insists he wouldn't just abandon Jackie and his children for someone else. And he insists that Jus has been happy with Jackie. He was stunned when I told him his friend had stayed two nights in Armonk. He's concerned, and I believe him." The two became thoughtful. The bright sun reflected off the ocean.

"Did you find out anything important?" Alexis was eager to hear from Travis. Now that the Aspen trip was over, she hoped they could move ahead looking for Justin. While in Colorado, she had decided to commit to the search. She called Jackie as soon as she got home to see if there had been any word.

"Yes and no." The two had developed a good rapport over the months. Travis thought he was learning his boundaries in dealing with her. He returned to the money trace.

"Justin withdrew five hundred thousand dollars in cash from a branch in Crystal City. The personal account, by the way, is the one that received the transfer from New York. Why do you suppose he moved the money so many times? Its origins appear to be from an overseas bank. But if the account was undeclared, he's now exposed to the IRS."

Alexis shook her head and frowned, "He wanted cash and decided to take it from an undisclosed account." She paused to think and then continued. "The maneuvering is a puzzle. As baffling as leaving his rifle in care of his friend when he didn't have to reveal his presence at all." Alexis wondered how big a bag would be needed to hold half a million dollars.

"Did you ask Jackie if she knew anything about the money?"

"I asked if she and Justin kept large sums of money in the house, and she said no. I decided you should be the one to probe the matter deeper." Alexis nodded agreement.

"Want more coffee?"

Alexis took a sip from her cup and grimaced. "This is cold." She shivered. "So am I." She got up from her chair. "Let's go inside."

They settled themselves in the warm kitchen. Alexis filled the mugs with hot coffee while Travis continued his report. "In the two weeks before he disappeared, Jus made three calls from his office and a couple from his home to an unlisted number out in Virginia. These turned out to be to his lawyer's residence. He also made calls to Mr. Lawyer's office in downtown D.C. I couldn't find out if they met. Jus doesn't keep all his appointments and meetings on his calendar. I didn't think I'd get anywhere calling the firm, and I didn't want anyone to know we're interested. You said Jackie told you the lawyer cautioned her against getting someone outside of the family involved in the matter."

"That's right. She did."

Travis got up from the table, walked to the window, and with his back to Alexis continued his narration. "The lawyer had left town with his wife for the holidays, and I decided to have our operatives put a tap on the residence. It was a little tricky, but not as bad as it would have been if they were home."

Alexis turned in her chair to look at Travis still looking out the window. Her body tensed, and she furred her brow in surprise. "Our operatives?"

"Yes. You know. The ones Lucas used on that case the summer before his accident. I know one of them from Desert Storm. Did I ever mention him? He learned most of the stuff with Intelligence and now works free lance. He doesn't know that I'm connected to you, if that concerns you."

Not waiting for a reply, Travis rushed on. "Obviously we didn't try for anything at the office but if there's any contact from Justin, it probably would be at the guy's home. Meanwhile, Jackie had the phone calling features you suggested installed to help identify and track callers. Do you think maybe we should put a tap on her phone as well?" Finally Travis gave way for Alexis' reaction.

"Travis! What do you think gave you the authority to make such decisions?" Alexis vented her anger. "You went to search the systems. Period." Setting a tap on the lawyer's residence was an ill-considered move, with potentially serious repercussions. Furthermore, Travis had ordered it without consulting her. She was sure he never mentioned a connection with the team he used. They had been used sparingly by Lucas, and in only the most difficult of circumstances, not for something on a hunch.

"I thought you might be pissed. The kind of trail I was picking up was faint enough. The guy has disappeared. If he's done it on purpose, he might have arranged for someone to cover him. The lawyer seems a good bet, and I had to make a quick decision."

Travis was uncomfortable with the confrontation. He wasn't convinced Jackie was telling Alexis everything. Although Jackie had agreed to give him full access to Justin's computers and records, she also insisted on staying with him while he searched. Phillip stayed close when he worked at the office. In addition, Jackie had been reluctant to provide the name and phone numbers of the family lawyer even though Travis assured her there would be no direct contact.

When asked, Jackie acknowledged that Justin had a luncheon scheduled at the country club with Louis the Sunday after the accident, a date Justin had been unable to keep. After that, Jackie said she knew of no meetings Justin may have had with Louis, and wasn't comfortable with his insistence that she not ask for outside help. However, she was adamant that Louis could not be in any way involved.

Is Jackie naïve, or does she have doubts about Louis she's unwilling to express? I think Alexis is too close to the situation. She didn't respond to the tap suggestion for Jackie. Would she have agreed to the one on the lawyer? Travis returned to the table prepared to defend his actions.

"We can't work that way." Alexis also had to make a quick decision: take care of the unauthorized actions now or do it when they were less pressed to act. She felt that Travis may be naturally insubordinate, and may not be easily persuaded to accept her authority. What was done was done, she reasoned. She decided to wait. Nevertheless, she was furious.

"We'll deal with your out-of-line actions later. Right now, get back to what you found out. Justin's unexplained behaviors start tracking from the trip to New York to meet Peter. Who is this Peter anyway? What do we know?"

"Justin received a call from a motel near LaGuardia just before he made his trip to meet Peter." Travis returned to his report. "The call which came so late that Friday night originated from Toronto. The next day, Saturday, a call to the Air Canada Center in Toronto, was made from Justin's office. Another call to the same number was made in late afternoon the day before Justin left for his hunting trip. Since we don't know Peter's last name, I could go up to Toronto and try to locate him by going to the center. He must be known if he had access to their phones. Do you know if Jus was into gambling?" He had asked that question before. "Maybe he's gotten in over his head."

"Maybe." Alexis frowned and thought back. "He talked once or twice about going to casinos in Europe and Vegas, but I've never heard anyone suggest he was excessive. Lucas never did. I don't know if going to Toronto is a good idea." Alexis didn't want to send Travis off again on his own, especially out of country. He was too impulsive, freewheeling. "Besides, Peter dates back to Berlin, and reappeared unexpectedly. I think some of the answers are in Berlin. I wonder if Anna would talk with me if I went there. She doesn't know me; I doubt she would tell me much over the phone."

"To Berlin?" Travis was surprised. This seemed an unexpected move based on the little they knew about Justin's meeting with Peter.

"You want to go before we know more about him in Toronto?" Travis knew Alexis was reluctant to send him off again. "I should be able to get a line on him without too much trouble. I may even locate him."

"Yes, Berlin." Alexis made the decision. As though it were a move not needing further discussion, she said, "Either way, I think there is much to find out in Berlin. You go to Toronto. I'll go to Germany. If you do locate him, don't approach him. Wait to discuss it with me." Travis, taken back with the abrupt end to the discussion, sat speechless as Alexis left the kitchen, already planning her trip.

* * *

In the late afternoon, Alexis sat in a lush leather chair in her office. She hesitated about asking Captain to return from St. Augustine so soon. Since Lucas' death, she had become closer to him, and appreciated the support he offered her and the children. Still, she suspected he didn't approve of her continuing the investigative side of the businesses she now operated on her own, and he was comfortable in Florida with his boat and pals. He actually admitted to having a lady friend who shared his love of sailing. Nothing serious, he assured her, but she hoped it was. *That's probably why he returned there for the New Year. Good for him. He's obviously lonely.*

Alexis got up, stretched, and began to pace, still deep in contemplation. Assuming Anna would agree to her visit, she didn't know how long she would be in Europe. In some respects, it was a long shot that she would uncover something useful which would shed light on Justin's behavior. Yet Alexis had a hunch that Justin's encounter with Karl in Dresden, and the sudden reappearance of Peter, was not coincidence. Like Jackie, who in her convoluted way had perceived a connection, she believed the two ocean separated meetings were related.

As circumstances stood, she and Travis were at a dead end as far as where next to look. But she couldn't leave the children with Maria for an extended time. Even with a power of attorney. It would be too much of a responsibility to place on her, especially since Travis also would be away.

Alexis sat at her desk. She put in a call to St. Augustine.

Chapter Six

The cold took his breath away as Travis left the airport terminal to pick up his rental car. Below freezing and overcast, he turned up the collar of his jacket and pulled out his gloves. A new front was moving in from the west.

Rush hour was just beginning as he reached the exit off the expressway at Spadina Avenue. Travis checked into the hotel only blocks from the Air Canada Center, spent a short time in his room, and then headed out. At first he had thought he would call the number obtained from Justin's phone records, but later decided a direct approach made better sense. That way he could get a feel for the situation and layout of the arena complex and also assess reactions face to face. Already becoming dark, it was too early for fans to start arriving, but he was certain to find employees preparing for the game that night. He was not certain if he would find out anything about Peter this late in the afternoon, but he wanted to start his quest.

Travis had pressed Alexis for the opportunity to come to Toronto, and knowing she had reservations, he was apprehensive about the outcome. Also, he realized she was still annoyed with him for arranging the phone tap on the lawyer without her approval. Of course, he admitted silently, that was why she had reservations.

Once at the center, Travis looked for a way in. All the entrance doors were locked, but through the glass he saw people walking briskly in all directions and carts waiting at elevators for transport to other levels. Descending the steps, he walked around the building until he found the service entrance. Delivery trucks were parked outside and employees were arriving for work.

Travis slipped through a door with two delivery men and sauntered to the elevator. He stepped in with three workers on the way up. He exited with the group and found himself on the main concourse which ran around the indoor stadium where the Maple Leafs hockey team was playing that night. Peering through an entrance leading to the vast arena of empty seats, Travis looked down to the playing area where an ice resurfacing machine with a sprinkler hose and cloth towel was preparing the ice. Methodically it moved across the arena laying down clean water to fill residual groves created by a shaving blade and forming a new ice surface. A hockey fan since his youth, Travis watched the activity with interest then turned back to the concourse.

Around him people were bustling at the concession sites setting up to serve the hungry fans. He walked over to a woman wearing a vendor badge, "Excuse me. I have an appointment at the operations office. Can you direct me?"

The woman stopped arranging sandwiches on the cart. "Take the elevator to the top floor. There'll be a sign."

"Thank you." Travis walked back to the elevator. Now that he was here, he felt the earlier apprehension. *This could take a bit of fast talk!*

On the top floor, seeing no sign, Travis entered an office. "May I help you?" a woman asked from her desk.

"I hope so." Travis flashed a smile he believed made him attractive to women. "I'm looking for a guy I met not long ago who works here. A guy named Peter." Still smiling, Travis moved closer to the desk.

"Peter what?"

Travis laughed, a bit embarrassed. "That's the problem. We talked together over a beer in New York and he forgot to tell me his last name, or I didn't catch it. He told me to look him up here at the center."

The woman looked at him and frowned. "A lot of people work here. Some of them are named Peter. Do you know what he does?"

"No. Just that he works here all kinds of different hours. This is the phone number he gave me to use if I called." Travis pulled out a small piece of paper containing the number from Justin's phone records.

"Just a minute. I'll see if I can help you." The woman walked to another desk where she checked a list and dialed a number. She talked to someone on the other end and waited. She spoke again, nodded her head, and then hung up. Returning to her desk, this time she smiled. "Larry in the concessions office may know who you're looking for. He said to come on over. Left out the door and down the hall. Another left and about half way. You'll see the sign."

Minutes later, Travis was talking with Larry. Feeling more confident with his story, Travis went through it again.

"Off hand, I couldn't say who it could be. Can you describe him?" Larry seemed cautious.

Travis took a shot. "Shorter than me, not too heavy, dark hair. He said he spent a long time in Germany a while back. Maybe Berlin."

Larry looked at Travis in silence, studying him while thinking. "That could be Peter Dominique," he said. "Peter's pretty much on the scrawny side, but did tell us he once worked in Europe." Larry studied Travis again then whirled around in his desk chair and went to a file cabinet.

"Peter worked here off and on with some of the concessions when the Maple Leafs and Raptors were in season. I think he also worked with cleanup. The thing is, he hasn't been around for awhile," Larry took out a file. "Didn't say he wouldn't be back. Just hasn't shown up."

"Really? About when was he here last? Two or three weeks ago?" Travis prompted trying to pin it down. Alexis and he wondered if Justin met Peter on his second trip to New York in November.

Larry scrutinized Travis more closely. Travis sensed suspicion. *What is this guy thinking? Did I push too hard?*

"More than that," Larry said. He thought a minute. "Before Christmas. Maybe even November. When did you say you ran into him?"

"October. In New York. We were laying over in a motel near LaGuardia and drank a couple beers together in a lounge. Like I said, I mentioned I'd be here sometime on business, and he told me to look him up."

"I don't know. He hasn't been around. Had a girl friend that dropped by once in a while when he was working. She was looking for him before Christmas. They shared a room or apartment near the University. You want the address?"

Travis thought about it quickly. Why would someone on a business trip continue to pursue the whereabouts of a casual acquaintance who told him to drop by when in town? At the same time, Larry now seemed more than eager to help. "Oh, I don't know. We were just going to get together for a drink. He said he may be able to fix me up with a ticket to a game." Larry was looking in the file.

"I guess I can take her name and address. If I have time, I could call her and let her know that Peter and I met. Maybe she's heard from him, or he's turned up and found another job."

Larry shrugged as he wrote down Mary's name and the rooming-house address. He handed the paper to Travis. "Mary Rochellle. I don't think she has a phone number. He didn't. Maybe there's one for the house.

"Peter sometimes made calls from here." Larry volunteered. "Got them too. People asking us to page him, no less. Can you believe that? Page him! Once someone went looking for him. Not me, though."

Travis put the paper in his coat pocket. "It sure takes all kinds. People are weird. Thanks for your help. I know this is a busy time."

"Big game tonight. Then we see all of them as big." Larry brightened up for the first time.

Travis laughed. "I know what you mean. Any chance a ticket's still available?"

"Possibly. What did you say your name is?"

"Travis." Up until now he had intentionally not identified himself, but Travis realized he had to respond, if only offering his first name.

"Let me call down, Travis. You can pick it up on your way out if there is. Game starts at seven thirty."

"I appreciate it."

Travis walked back to his hotel with a ticket in his wallet. He was excited by the fact that he had a last name for Peter and decided to pass it on to Alexis at once. He sent out an e-mail hoping she had not yet left for Berlin. Later he returned to the arena.

Snow and strong wind had moved in during the night. Travis waited until noon to call the rooming house. No one answered. After a short wait, he tried again. Still no answer. Sighing with annoyance, Travis pulled on a sweater, threw on his coat, and went down to catch a taxi.

Mary was a part-time student working in the side bar of a restaurant in Little Italy not far from the Skydome. The concierge of the rooming house gave Travis directions. She was a pretty girl he thought, although she looked wan and pale.

When Travis first approached Mary, she seemed startled and resistant. Yet it took little convincing to have her take a break and join him for coffee and a sandwich in the adjoining grill. They were hardly seated when a customer came in and took a booth not far from where they were sitting.

Mary seemed nervous. "You say you know Peter?"

"Only slightly. We met a few months ago in New York. He said to look him up when I got here. Offered to point the way to good restaurants. I was looking for him at the center yesterday, and Larry gave me your name and rooming house address."

"Are you his friend from Berlin?"

"Me? Oh no. I met him in New York. It was in a lounge at the motel where we were staying near the airport." Travis tried not to show his interest at her statement about Berlin.

Mary's eyes welled up with tears. "He hasn't been back since he made the second trip in November. I think something terrible has happened. He really didn't want to go. He was getting more work at the arena and at the boat place. Making more money. It was inconvenient."

Travis was stuck. He had confirmed Peter's last name and now a positive link to Justin. He hoped this would vindicate his push to make the trip to Toronto.

"I don't know what to say. I'm sorry." They sat there in silence. Mary wiped her eyes and tried a smile. She was a good-looking girl, warm and just nice. Travis wondered if Peter was a rat.

"I'm sorry to be so weepy. It's just that I thought maybe you would to be able to tell me something that could explain what happened."

"I don't think I can. I mean, we met near the end of October and you say he went again in November. Did these two guys have something a little," he hesitated, "well, sort of a scam going, maybe? I mean I don't want to suggest Peter's a crook or anything. Maybe playing an angle. You know." The dialogue made Travis feel like a jerk.

"I just don't know. Peter's a love, but he's not a saint. It all seemed to happen after he began doing a little work for Raffi at the harbor. Peter said a man looked him up at the arena and offered him some part-time work. The man said Makhmud, who owns some of the concessions, knew about him. Makhmud also owns the boat works down in the inner harbor."

"Why do you think the trips were connected to his job at the boat works?" Noise from the bar area hiked up as a group of students burst in.

"Because he changed after he started there. He was tense for some reason. Wouldn't talk as much. Then suddenly, he said he was making a trip to New York to look up an old friend from Berlin. Said this man had gotten in touch with him, and wanted to see him. Sent him money to make the trip. I thought it sounded crazy, but Peter's very sensitive and defensive. He doesn't like to be questioned too closely. He . . . He's had a hard time the past few years." She hesitated, as though not willing to say more. "So I tried to make it seem okay. When he came back the tension was gone and he was his old self, but then he left again." Mary struggled to keep her composure.

Out of the corner of his eye, Travis caught the careful scrutiny of the man in the nearby booth. Mary seemed genuine in her distress. *Does she know that guy?* Travis was sure he was being watched. He reached a comforting hand across to Mary and gently squeezed her arm. "I really am sorry. It sounds like crap. I wish I could tell you more, but I just don't know anything."

"I know. I appreciate you trying to help." She took a deep breath and wiped her face again. "I'd better go freshen up. I need to get back to work."

"Finish your coffee and sandwich. You don't need to say more. Relax a few more minutes." He smiled reassuringly. "You happen to have some photos of you and Peter?"

Mary looked surprised through her teary eyes. "A couple." She took out a wallet and showed Travis some snapshots: Mary and a slender man with dark hair standing near the water, another of the two seated at an outside café. Peter had managed a smile in the second.

"Do you have one you can spare?"

"Oh no. Not these."

"That's okay. I know they're special. I just thought I could use one to help me recognize Peter again or show it to others who might know him. If I have a chance." Travis glanced over at the man in the booth.

"I have some at my apartment I could let you have, but not now. I have to work." Mary put away her wallet.

"If I give you a stateside address, could you send me one? I won't bother you again this trip."

"Sure." Mary drained her cup and wiped her mouth. She looked at Travis with new interest.

Travis reached over for an unused napkin and quickly wrote his address. He picked up the check and got out money to leave a tip on the table. He wrapped a bill in the napkin and handed it to Mary. "It doesn't have to be a special one. A good shot of his face would do."

Travis called a cab and stood outside to wait. The man in the booth left at the same time, paid his check, and walked up the block. Feigning disinterest, Travis watched him get in the passenger side of a waiting car. Rather than pull away, it stayed parked.

Travis thought about his meeting with Mary. He was disturbed and confused by her narration. According to Peter's story, Justin initiated the contact and desire for a meeting. Even sent him money. According to Jackie, Justin received an unexpected phone call which was compelling enough that he made a sudden trip to New York. Justin received the call from a motel near LaGuardia. And what about the second trip by Peter to New York in November? A cab pulled up. The car down the street had not moved. "Down to Harbor Square, please."

Driving through the traffic was slow, but this gave him time to think. Travis knew he no longer could continue the ruse of a business trip if he tried to track down Makhmud or Raffi at the boat works. The encounter would break his cover and acknowledge his real purpose. Did he want to do this?

Travis shifted his position to gain vantage to the rear view mirrors. His musings continued. Peter was missing. Travis was not going to find him here in Toronto. What might he gain by following the lead to Makhmud? He suspected that Peter worked for some dangerous people, possibly connected to drugs. What activities are being shielded by the harbor boat works owned by the shadowy Makhmud? 'Makhmud owns some of the concessions,' Mary had explained. What else did he sell besides sandwiches and beer? The day was turning colder. Gusts of wind blew litter in the gutters. They approached the CN Tower.

Mary's story didn't track, Travis concluded. Was Peter's connection to Makhmud also a connection to his contact and business with Justin? Maybe Makhmud and his men also were looking for Peter. Then again, maybe they knew why Peter was missing and were responsible.

Travis looked into the driver's rear view. A couple of cars back he thought he caught a glimpse of the one he noted at the restaurant. The taxi was passing the Kensington Market. Action outside was subdued in the February cold, but the colorful and diverse character of the neighborhood was noticeable nonetheless.

Travis continued his analysis. Maybe Peter's connection with Makhmud was totally unrelated to the contact Peter made with Justin. Maybe he should go back to his hotel as though he let the matter drop after leaving Mary. Keep his cover. Go back to D.C. Then again, if he approached the people at the boat works, he might get a better picture of what Peter's contact with Justin was all about. Surely it was more involved than just a guy looking up an old acquaintance from years ago.

For the next few blocks Travis mulled it over, uncertain what to do. He had lobbied hard to get this trip. He felt he was on the verge of exceeding more than he had hoped to accomplish. The taxi turned on Queen Street and a few blocks further again on Blue Jay Way. They definitely were being followed by the other car. The taxi passed the restaurant owned by Wayne Gretsky.

Travis spoke to the driver. "I hear that's a choice place to eat."

"Great atmosphere too. Sometimes Wayne is there although I don't think he's in town now."

"I was at the game last night. Terrific. Did you catch the hat trick?"

"Sure did. Watched on TV."

Travis decided to evaluate the situation more before taking action. I've changed my mind. Make it the Princess Royal." First he had to shake the tail. It must be the result of a tip from Larry. For now there was no need for anyone to know where he was staying.

"Sure thing."

Travis paid the driver. A quick glance showed his tail had pulled up only a couple lengths behind. He entered the lobby moving slowly in order to see that the man from the restaurant followed.

Travis went straight to the elevators. He and one other person entered when the doors opened. The man pushed three, and Travis pushed ten.

At the third floor, Travis exited with the other guest and looked for the stairs. The elevator continued to the tenth floor.

Travis descended quickly and came out at the far side of the lobby. He ducked through a side entrance into a sidewalk full of pedestrians. Turning away from the direction of the hotel front, he walked quickly through the deepening gloom of late afternoon. He returned to the Plaza.

* * *

A little after two the next afternoon, Travis drove down to the inner harbor area in search of the boat works described by Mary. She had told him it was not far from the yacht club. According to the city map, there were two clubs, but they were located close to one another. By now, there had been enough time for the employees at the boat works to expect him, but Travis had waited until after lunch time to be sure someone would be minding the store.

Driving slowly along Queens Quay, Travis pulled out of traffic and idled at the curb. He rolled down a window and hailed a couple of guys on the street. "I'm looking for the yacht club. Am I close?"

One of the men walked to the car. "There's one just down the street a couple of blocks. Turn left at the next light."

"Thanks." Travis raised the window and pulled back into traffic. After making the turn, he slowly cruised down the street and stopped close to a fenced area with a small building fronting an enclosed boat house. By its size, Travis estimated it to contain two work bays. He parked across from the building. The area was quiet with little traffic.

Travis locked the car and walked toward the building. Glancing upward, he noticed surveillance cameras monitoring several angles on the street. *Why so much security?*

Knowing he was being watched, Travis walked over to look through the fence. Moored at the end of an outside dock he spotted a pleasure yacht. He turned toward the entrance of the building. With his danger instincts on alert, Travis wasn't convinced this visit was the best move, but he was committed.

The front part of the building was a chandlery with an office at the back. Through an open door Travis caught a glimpse of a room which he guessed had another entrance to the work bays. The store was empty when he entered, although he could hear activity out behind the building through the adjoining room. A man with Asian features appeared. "What you want?" he asked with a thick accent.

"I'm looking for Makhmud."

"Not here. You have business?"

"I'm looking for someone and was told Makhmud might be able to help. Will he be here anytime soon?" The man looked at Travis without comment. There was a slight noise from the other room.

Travis leaned casually on the counter and smiled. His glance swept the area on the wall behind and to the side looking for a surveillance camera. "I was told that Peter Dominique sometimes does small jobs here, part-time work." He wondered if this was Raffi.

"Why you want Peter? He in trouble?"

Travis shifted a little so he could discreetly take in other parts of the room. He glimpsed a recessed camera, probably with sound he thought. A couple of motion detectors were mounted in two locations, all part of a sweeping security system. *Nice place. Bet it's in all the buildings. Hello, low crime rate Toronto.* "Not that I know of. Do you know Peter? Maybe you can help."

"I know Peter. He not here for long time." The guy wasn't giving an inch. He looked at Travis and waited.

This was where Travis had to give it away or cut altogether. He realized that by his very presence, they knew he wasn't here looking for a casual contact. Travis notched up his danger awareness. At a minimum he had been under surveillance from the time he approached the office. Maybe earlier. He thought about the distance to his car.

"Peter met with a friend in New York back in October. That man left his wife and family suddenly in November and hasn't been heard from. The wife asked me to look for him. I want to ask Peter about their meeting to see if it will help find the husband." He spoke slowly for the man to understand. *Shit. There it is. Now what?* The early afternoon dusk had started to close. Travis didn't think he was a threat to these people, but he knew he was in a dangerous situation.

"Wait." The man turned and walked to the back room. Travis could hear a low discussion taking place. No sign of anyone in the area outside the windows. The chandlery room was eerily quiet. He had a sense of time suspended. A phone rang. More low muttering. Travis couldn't tell if they were speaking English. He made no attempt to get close to the door. He sensed his every move was being watched by cameras. *Play it casual. Don't be too interested.*

The man reappeared, his demeanor unchanged. "Makhmud on boat. He say he talk with you. Come. I take you." It was a short walk from the office to the dock leading to the tied boat. "Makhmud inside." Raffi pointed to the boat. "He not know where Peter, but tell what he know. You tell about wife man." He turned back toward the office.

They want to know about Justin? So they are involved in Peter's contact with him. Warily Travis advanced down the docking area. He felt dangerously exposed. If Peter and Justin were involved with drugs, these guys might see him as someone investigating their operation. He could be viewed as a threat after all. "Hello. Coming aboard." It was when Travis stepped on the ramp to the boat that he spied a gunman in the recessed stairs to the upper deck. He lunged on board and flattened himself against the cabin wall. At the same time he heard the poof of a silencer as a slug hit the ramp.

Slipping out of his coat, Travis dove over the side. The water was frigid; he felt his clothes clinging and weighting him down. Angling sharply, he slowly rose toward the surface in the murky water.

Travis believed he was at the end of the keel and confirmed this with a touch. He edged towards the propeller and quietly put his head above the surface. Although out of sight, he knew he couldn't stay long in the cold water. Sounds from the boat deck above were audible. *I could use my wet suit about now.* He slipped off his shoes. Shivering, he mentally reviewed the location of the boat in relation to the surrounding water front and considered his options. *Shit. I've got to move. Get out of range and out of the water in that order.* He ducked down once more under the water.

Minutes later a man working on his boat in the nearby yacht club helped Travis clambered aboard, icy water splashing on the deck. "Thanks," he gasped.

Without comment the man hustled Travis quickly into the small cabin. Out of the cold, Travis welcomed the rush of warm air. The boater pulled a blanket off a bunk and reached into a closet for a towel. "Get out of your clothes. I've got pants and a sweat shirt you can use."

Once dry and dressed, Travis offered an abbreviated explanation to his rescuer. "Over there," he pointed vaguely, "one of the guys at the boat works and I had a difference of opinion that got out of hand."

"Looks that way." The yachtsman Tom Cross said with raised eyebrow as he gave Travis an appraising look. "You want to call the police or harbor patrol?"

"Not just yet, if you don't mind. It's complicated. I'd like to get back to my hotel first and pull myself together." Tom handed him a mug of coffee laced with brandy. With the first gulp, Travis felt a surge of warmth. He wondered if Makhmud's men would come looking for him.

Rather than question him too closely, Tom gave Travis a ride to the hotel. Before Travis got out, he handed him a paper with a name and phone number. "If you have a chance, send the clothes to me at the yacht club."

"Absolutely. I can't tell you how much I appreciate your help." *Is he going to report the incident?*

"Glad I was there to pull you aboard." Tom laughed for the first time. "Let me know if you need anything more. My wife would probably find you fascinating."

Back in his room, Travis vigorously rubbed down, took a long hot shower, and, wrapped in the hotel robe, sat under the blanket. He ordered room service and waited hungrily for the food. The past couple of hours had been a nightmare.

Travis began thinking about getting out of Toronto. He believed Makhmud and accomplishes knew where he was in spite of his weaving and dodging the day before. If not, they would soon by searching the rental car with the agreement in the glove compartment. He was shaken by the severity of the attack. It was going to take a while to calm down. *Right now, though, I'm starving.*

Not far away, lights were dark at Makhmud's boat house; the doors to the two work bays were closed, and the moorings at the end of the back dock were empty.

Chapter Seven

Anna was surprised when Alexis called from North Carolina. Surprised, and then hesitant. She remembered hearing of Alexis from her sons and was sorry to hear about Lucas, whom she had met once when he was in Berlin. No, she didn't know he left the navy and had become a private investigator. She commented on Alexis' fluent German, and acknowledged approval when told Alexis now working on her own as an investigator. Uncertain as to why she was being called, Anna suggested they switch to English, noting that she was comfortable in either language. When Anna heard about Justin's disappearance and that Alexis was assisting in the effort to find him, she became cautious.

"I haven't heard from, nor spoken to Justin for several years. He's disappeared? Do you mean he just suddenly didn't come home one day?" *Why hasn't Phillip or Mathias mentioned this? Certainly Phillip knows.*

"It's a bit more complicated than that, although we're not entirely sure about all the circumstances. A colleague and I are working from what information Jackie has given us, and we've spoken with some friends."

"That's interesting," Anna replied in a caustic tone. "Justin has a habit of being involved in complicated situations. Does Philip know? Of course he does, he's right there. Do you think it's another woman?"

Several thousand miles away, Alexis smiled. "We haven't ruled that out, but it isn't what circumstances point to." *I think I'm going to like this woman.*

"Are you calling because you think I know anything about where he is? I haven't had contact with Justin since he visited with Matthias in Frankfurt three or four years ago. I heard he was in Germany last fall, but I don't think he came here, and he certainly didn't call. I don't know how I can be of any help."

"Anna," Alexis began her pitch, "a Berlin acquaintance of Justin's from the eighties made contact with him a few month's back, a person by the name of Peter. Do you remember meeting someone by that name?" Anna did not respond.

"Hello?"

Finally Anna replied in a cautious voice. "Peter. I recall a Peter with whom Justin had some dealings. I can't imagine why he would get in touch with Justin now. It's been years since they last saw one another, as far as I know." *When was Peter released from prison?*

"Do you remember his last name?" Alexis pressed.

"Umm. Well, let me think. It was French I think. He was French-Canadian as I remember. He worked in the British zone."

She sounds worried. For some reason, the mention of Peter is disturbing. Alexis waited for a reply.

"Dominique, I think. Peter Dominique," Anna finally said.

Yes! Alexis cheered to herself. *A full name. Good!* "Peter Dominique. You say they had some business together?"

Anna was reluctant to discuss more on the phone. "I don't think I can tell you much. Both of them worked for post exchange services, Justin for the Americans, Peter for the British. Their positions weren't comparable, and I don't think they had much contact. I may have met Peter once. It's vague after all this time."

Alexis felt Anna's hesitance. "I realize this is unexpected. I apologize for surprising you." She wondered how often Philip was in touch with his mother. Justin's disappearance probably was not a topic he'd call her about, given the family's past. Yet she was surprised that Anna had not been informed. Philip was, after all, the one who provided her with Anna's phone number. "I wanted to make initial contact with you today, but feel you may be more comfortable discussing this matter with me in person."

"In person? Do you mean you want to come here?" *If Alexis is ready to come to Berlin, Justin's disappearance must be more involved that his roving eye for women.*

"If you will meet with me, that's what I have in mind. I can imagine you may not want to discuss some aspects of your life with Justin on the phone."

After a small silence, Anna made a reply that was more receptive than before, "I'll be glad to meet with you. You are correct, Alexis, I will not discuss much on the phone, especially not knowing you. However, if it will help, I wish to do what I can." She added, "My mother is living here with me now. Perhaps she can offer you something useful as well."

Anna's new willingness to assist once she heard Alexis would make a trip to Berlin was encouraging. That the mother might have something of value to say sounded even more promising. Alexis realized there must be quite a story waiting in Berlin. "That will be fine. I'll look forward to meeting her. If we agree then, I'll make arrangements and will be back in touch about my arrival."

* * *

West Berlin: Late fall 1986

When Peter first proposed the arrangement, Justin rejected it out of hand. "No way. If I got caught smuggling out drugs, I'd rot out my life in some prison in East Germany or Leavenworth." It was a scene Justin often relived in his mind.

"But you won't get caught. Your passage through the East side will be paved, and your people aren't looking for stuff coming this way from tourists and regulars. They know you make the trips to your mother-in-law."

"I think it's crazy. I can't take that kind of a risk." Justin knew Peter was connected to the seamy Berlin underworld, but he hadn't known about the drugs. *I should have suspected it. Maybe I ought to cut operations and contact with Peter.* It had been almost a year since he began stealing electronics out of the inventory at the PX, which Peter then sold on the black market.

For a couple of weeks, Peter kept working on him, and when the price reached two hundred thousand a trip, Justin gave in. They were talking in a noisy, smoky bierstube in the Kreuzberg district. "Okay. We'll do a dry run and I'll see. Who's going to do the car?"

"Why a dry run?" Peter looked smug at his coup. "If we go to the trouble of fixing up the car, we should get right to it. They won't want to run their people for nothing. Every activity means possible exposure. A few in the Stasi are in on it already."

"See. It's not that sure."

"For their people, a serious concern. For you, with your cover, almost nothing."

"But how will I recognize who is handling things on the checkpoint? How will they know which garage?"

"The neighborhood has been cased out, and they've been in the garage. The officer on the checkpoint is ready. You let me know a couple days or so in advance of your trip.

"You know both sides are primed mostly over controlling merchandise going in and people coming out so with the right person on the checkpoint, it won't be such a big deal. The Politzei watch the German crossings for drugs. Trust me."

"*Right.*" *God. I don't like it. I'm a fool to get mixed up with this kind of business.* Justin looked around the room. A workers' hangout. He imagined every other person to be part of Peter's network.

"Two hundred thousand a trip. That's a good payment." Peter touched Justin's beer mug in toast. "In Deutsch marks. The setup is perfect as long as we can keep the officer at the checkpoint in place."

One day on the way to work, Justin left the car outside the gates to the base. It was waiting for him that afternoon, parked under a tree in the quiet neighborhood nearby. When he got home, he looked carefully over the entire car. It took him over an hour to find the compartment. It was a masterful job. He thought about the briefings he had sat through, and the displays and films on smuggling and escapes from East Berlin at the Checkpoint Charlie Museum. He felt reassured but still was nervous.

* * *

Alexis picked up her bags and passed through customs. She was excited to be back in Berlin, although the trip was not for pleasure. She had heard about the many changes since her visit in 1989, just after the Wall came down. Then, she and Lucas had carried their hammer and chisel in a pack, and with friends chipped off their pieces, later passed through the Friedrichstrasse U Bahn station previously closed to anyone but Germans. The next year, before they left Europe, they came back. Even then, with Germany united, Berlin was undergoing vast transformation, and she was eager to see what had been accomplished.

Driving out of the airport in a taxi, she immediately could tell the difference. The traffic not only was as bad as ever, it was many times worse. Alexis, fighting jet lag, reminded herself of the hazards of the fast European driving, and congratulated her decision not to rent a car. *What a race track! It's worse than the D.C. to Richmond corridor. Welcome back to Formula One!* She almost ducked as a Mercedes flew past.

Alexis checked into the Kimpinski Berlin where she and Lucas had stayed those earlier exciting times. She had almost opted for the rebuilt Adlon to savor a bit of history, but decided to save that for another time. She would bring the children when they were older.

Once in her room, Alexis unpacked and took a hot shower. The long overnight flight and morning connection to Berlin had left her feeling tired and grungy. She never slept well on planes, and the six hours difference in time meant she had arrived in Frankfurt at two AM her time on the East Coast. To combat jet lag and ease the effects of long hours of sitting, she stretched out on the bed for a short nap. Later she bundled up and set out for a brisk walk.

The January winter air was frigid; a wind was blowing from the east. Alexis reminded herself that she was in Central Europe, and not in temperate North Carolina. She looked around for a direction to walk and decided to take a taxi to the Brandenberg Gate. Alexis wanted to recapture the feeling she had after the fall of the Berlin Wall. She also wanted to see the changes that had taken place along the path of the former Wall, particularly at Potsdamer Plaz, where frantic construction had replaced an empty no mans land.

When she stepped from the cab, Alexis thought she had been brought to the wrong place. Accustomed to having her view blocked by the Wall, she was astonished to find herself looking directly into the former East sector where building and reconstruction were both completed as well as ongoing. The sight was at first difficult to comprehend. *Lucas, if only you could see this!* Her thoughts flew back to the accounts about the post World War Berlin she had studied and listened to while growing up: Berlin situated alone and surrounded deep inside East Germany, Berlin in August 1961 when, in an effort to stop the increasing flight of citizens into the West, the Wall was thrown up in the dead of night.

Across the unobstructed vista she imagined Bernauerstrasse, which had bordered the Russian and French sector not far away beyond the Mitte district. Three days after the initial barrier had gone up, installation of concrete slabs began. Here seventeen-year-old VOPO, Volkspolizei, Conrad Schumann leaped across the wire and defected to the West. The act became a new symbol of Cold War reality.

So long ago. Forgotten or seldom thought about. Alexis hugged herself and rubbed her arms. It was cold standing there in the wind. The trees so green and full in summer were bare and stark against the winter sky. Moving quickly, she walked through the Brandenburg Gate and strolled down Unter den Linden. She decided to skip Potsdamer Platz, and walk to Checkpoint Charlie by way of Friedrichstrasse in what had been East Berlin.

Walking briskly, Alexis was mesmerized by the changes along what was previously a drab and depressing street with bullet-pocked buildings. She passed new restaurants, bookstores, and souvenir shops, and was surprised to look into a window display of Benetton.

The appearance of the street was so different that Alexis missed the fact that she had crossed the area which once was no mans land, past the spot where the Wall once stood, past the location of the East German and American crossing controls. In the middle of the street a reconstructed guard shack was surrounded by sandbags. She stood transfixed and spent several minutes to take it all in. *This is where Justin and American tourist crossed over to visit the East sector. It is as if that earlier time had never been!*

* * *

West Berlin: 1986

Justin had crossed through Checkpoint Charlie several times over the years. It was a routine trip that had caused him little concern. The first time he went for a drug shipment, however he was nervous and full of apprehension.

He approached the crossing by way of Wilhelm Strasse turning on Koch Strasse. Not far away the Wall loomed high and forbidding. American military patrols were cruising the area. Tourist who planned to cross on foot milled about, some of them just emerging from the nearby U Bahn station. Although he knew it was the return trip that would be the test, Justin felt light headed, his heart raced, and his shirt was damp with perspiration. *This is going to be a hell of a day!* It was the first of six trips. After the sixth, Peter was arrested.

* * *

Still lost in her reverie, Alexis turned and walked a short distance down Zimmerstrasse to the spot where a marker had been placed noting the death of a person killed while making a dash to cross to the West. The graffiti decorated slabs topped with barbed wire were gone. Years ago after the concrete barrier went up, eighteen year-old Peter Fechter climbed the wire fence on the East border, dashed across what was called the death strip, and almost reached safety before being shot by East German guards. One hundred fifty meters away at Checkpoint Charlie, U.S. army patrols were ordered to stay on their side of the border. Peter Fecter bled to death and was dragged away by the VOPOS. The fact that the Americans had done nothing to save the young man caused deep resentment and criticism by West Berliners. Now the street was quiet and all that remained of the earlier storm of despair was the marker.

Winter dusk ushered in early shadows over the subdued streets. Cold and feeling the effects of her emotions, Alexis walked back to the nearby Checkpoint Charlie Museum. In a little café next door she ordered a cup of coffee. A bit revived, she decided she had seen enough for one day, caught a taxi, and returned to the hotel.

Back in the warmth of the Kimpinski, Alexis phoned Anna, who answered after several rings. "Anna, this is Alexis. I've arrived in Berlin. Will there be a time soon when we can meet?"

"It's good to hear you've arrived safely. Were there any problems with the flight?"

"None at all. Everything went well. I made my connection from Frankfurt with time to spare. I've just come in from a walk, and I'm amazed at the changes that have occurred here since my last visit."

Anna laughed. "Yes, there has been a great deal of building as well as many changes throughout the city since you were here in eighty-nine."

"Would you like to come here to the Kimpinski for lunch tomorrow?" Alexis was eager to hear what Anna would reveal about Justin and Peter Dominique.

"No, I'm sorry." Anna replied. "I will not be at home until the afternoon. Can you come to the apartment at fifteen-thirty? We can talk over coffee and *kuchen*. My mother will be here as well."

Disappointed she would have to wait so long, Alexis replied, "That will be fine. It will give me time to rest up from the trip. I look forward to meeting you both. What is the address? I'll come by taxi."

Once they hung up, Alexis, eager to get news from Travis, checked her e-mail, but there were no updates. She sent a message to Captain and her children telling them of her arrival in Berlin. Feeling the effects of her outing in the cold, Alexis ordered a light meal to her room. Giving in to jet lag, she went to bed early.

Chapter Eight

The next day, Anna waited for Alexis' arrival in the large second-floor Dahlem apartment where she had raised her family. At the time she married Justin, she was living there and working for Siemens.

Anna was apprehensive about Alexis' visit, and kept peering from a window looking for her guest. She had worked hard to put behind her the disappointing aspects of the life she once shared with Justin, and wasn't looking forward to revisiting them with a stranger. At the same time, her sons had encouraged her to talk openly with Alexis, particularly Philip in a recent trans-Atlantic call.

Once Alexis arrived, the two women chatted together getting to know one another and merging their past. Anna asked about the circumstances that led to Lucas' death, and how Alexis was coping and adjusting. Alexis listened to Anna's childhood tale of separation, years of reunion with her mother, only to be separated again by a wall.

"My father was an international import-export business man, with many connections throughout Europe. We lived in Hamburg, and only after the war did my mother learn of the apartment my father owned here where he kept a mistress." Anna smiled woman to woman as she swept her hand around the richly paneled room and high ceiling with ornately carved trim, showing it off. Tall windows on the front admitted pale winter light.

"It's a lovely apartment, and the location is exceptional." Alexis was sincere.

"Let me show you some of the rooms." Anna led Alexis towards the dining area. "In July 1939, when I was two," she continued her story as they slowly moved through the apartment, "my father took the family to England for a visit with my aunt. She was married to a British exporter and lived outside of London. After a few weeks, papa returned to Hamburg. While the rest of us continued our vacation in England, Germany invaded Poland."

Anna paused at the entrance to a den furnished with overstuffed chairs, a couch, and a TV. "My mother was torn between concern for my older brother and me, and her concern for papa. Mutti returned to Germany expecting to bring us home when the situation cleared up, but before she could arrange for our return, it was too late. Ralf and I spent the war in England. When papa was called to fill a position in the government they moved to Berlin. In early 1945, he was killed in a bombing raid near the central city."

The two women entered the kitchen where Anna poured hot coffee into a karaffe and moved a plate of pastries to the table. Alexis was intently caught up with the narration. "When did you return to Berlin?"

"Ralf and I were reunited with Mutti and our younger brother Albert in the summer of 1946 even though she lived in the Russian zone." Anna shook her head at the memory. "In 1962, when the Wall went up, Ralf and I were living in this apartment and Mutti was cut off in East Berlin with Albert. I remained here alone when Ralf moved to Nürnburg." She finished her account, and looked at her watch.

"Please excuse me," Anna finished setting the tray. "I will rouse Mutti from her nap. Will you carry the cups and coffee into the living room?" Alexis noted Anna's effort to keep the meeting informal by including her in the preparation.

When Anna returned, she sat and poured them each a cup of coffee. "Please help yourself to the kuchen. My mother will join us shortly. What is it I can tell you about Justin and Peter?"

Alexis was taken off guard by the change of topic. "I'm not sure. You implied that the two had some dealings together." *Let her open the doors!*

Anna gave Alexis a long searching look. She wondered if she was ready to be candid about Justin. "The seventies and eighties here, things here were, well let us say wide open. West Berlin was an island surrounded by a hostile government, almost like a hostage. Yet, supported by the West German government, and with the military presence of the three allies, it recovered from the war and flourished. Do you want to hear my perception of the time, or only about Justin?"

"I think I should hear how you saw the times and how Justin fit into them." Alexis gently prodded.

Anna paused to think. "The atmosphere was always charged by the presence of a full range of political groups." She looked at Alexis who nodded encouragement. "Young people flocked here to live and study, exempted from obligatory German military service. They constantly participated in street demonstrations, most of them calling for peace and co-existence. They were anti-military and anti-U.S. The Amies, Brits, and French troops and their families added to the mix. So did the Russians, who were just beyond the Wall, the DDR military, and the Stasi. Spies were everywhere and people were ransomed out from the East in exchange for hard currency. Tourists flocked here to experience the unusual situation, and get a controlled, but titillating, peek at the East. Without a doubt, it was an exciting city." Anna looked at Alexis, and got up to stand looking out a window at the winter sky approaching twilight. Her back was to Alexis who couldn't read her face, but Anna's tone was somber.

"Along with the youth, intrigue, exciting music, and rising affluence, drugs were a pervasive presence, which was accompanied by aggressive crime. Our isolated situation intensified the sense of urgency to live to the fullest." Anna paused and turned to face Alexis who was listening with close attention.

"I was here in the seventies with my parents, and then twice with Lucas after the Wall came down." Alexis felt she needed to make some reply. *Where is this leading?* "I remember some of what you describe. The first time I was in my teens. Demonstrations filled the streets and I found it exciting. As you say, taking the tour to the East was memorable."

Anna smiled knowingly. "Justin, the children, and I were living a comfortable life. He was excellent at his job, paid well, had investments, and received other benefits, including exchange and commissary privileges. I had my own position. Yet, you remember how many people acted and thought then," she said in a tone Alexis heard as contempt, "'Greed is good' and Justin was accustomed to flamboyant and risky behaviors."

Leaning against the windowsill, Anna reluctantly concluded, "For a man like Justin, I think it was hard to resist trying to get a 'piece of the action', as he called it. Can you understand what I'm saying?"

* * *

West Berlin: January 1988

Justin was nervous. "Peter, I don't think we should do it again so soon. It's only been two months. Someone is bound to get suspicious of the frequent trips to my mother-in-law, particularly my wife." They were sitting in the Kreuzburg bierstube where they always met. Cigarette smoke hovered over the tables filled with swarthy men dressed in drab gray work clothes and scruffy boots. Black wool jackets hung on the chairs. Justin had been getting concerned about the repeated visits. *We ought to move around some, so we won't be recognized.*

Peter signaled for another beer. "Every trip has gone smoothly. Prices are up; my connections want to step up their distribution. And competition is growing." He leaned back in his chair, giving Justin close scrutiny. "You haven't lost your nerve have you?"

"Some." Justin admitted, thinking maybe this would get Peter to lay off a little. "There are rumblings about investigations into losses out of the exchange. I think we've got to cool it on all counts. No more stuff from the PX for awhile. No more runs to the East. Everything that goes on is getting crazier over there."

Peter laughed. "That only makes it easier. Karl is well positioned. His contacts are careful. But you may be right about the exchange. I've been hearing rumors over at ours as well. I bet too many people have their fingers in the pie." He laughed again. "Make the run on Saturday. You'll see it's okay." He took a long pull on his beer and wiped his mouth with the back of his hand.

* * *

Anna resumed her seat, and warmed up their cup. She motioned to the plate of pastries urging Alexis to help herself to more.

She continued, "I don't know when Justin started his dealings with Peter. After we married in 1971, he was transferred from Frankfurt to Berlin." Alexis slowly lifted her fork and looked intently at Anna. She sensed she was about to hear what she had traveled so far to discover.

"I think it was mid-eighties when Justin began to be restless, almost bored. He was as high as he could rise with AAFES without leaving Berlin. At some point, he and Peter began stealing electronic items from the Post Exchange inventory. Then Peter sold them on the black market. Some of it, I'm sure went to the East, although there was a ready market for it here. From what I read later in the *Stars and Stripes*, Peter was stealing from the British post as well. It came out he was a big operator."

Anna sipped her coffee, keeping her eyes fixed on the table. "Justin was only one of a number in Peter's network. That might have been what saved Jus, since there were others in the PX doing the same thing at the same time. Peter also was accused of smuggling Deutsch marks into the East. As far as I ever saw, there was never anything about drugs, but that could have been was part of it. What happened to my mother at her house after Justin's trip must have been a result of his connection to

Peter. It occurred during the winter of nineteen eighty-eight at the time of Peter's arrest."

Alexis looked startled. Anna smiled. "Didn't you know? I think Lucas did." She considered carefully, "Of course, the IG never definitively linked Justin to the missing inventory, although he was relocated to Dallas while they completed the investigation. By then, Peter was in prison. I remained here so Matthias could finish his senior year in high school. At first, Justin believed he would be reinstated and would return to us."

Alexis held up her hand. "Wait. You're right. I'm shocked. Lucas suggested once that Justin left here under a cloud of some kind of wrongdoing, but he never said what it was. Justin stole goods from the exchange and sold them on the black market?" *Good grief! I wonder if Jackie knows. Surely not.*

"In a word, yes." Anna had given careful thought about how and what she would disclose to Alexis. "I don't know exactly how the items were taken or how the records were covered up, but, yes." She took a deep breath. Alexis thought she could detect tears welling in Anna's eyes.

"In the beginning, I don't think that Justin actually thought of himself as a thief. I think he was challenged by the risk, and thought it was only fair that he share in the profits from the flourishing illicit activity. Fortunately or unfortunately, he was more careful than others who got caught: GIs working part time, Germans working for the Army, other managers, even school officials and teachers. If only it had ended with that! But Justin couldn't resist being pulled into worse." Anna stopped and stood up.

"Here's my mother," she smiled at the elderly woman entering the room. She switched to German, and moved to make a place for her to share the afternoon coffee.

. . . "Of course, I was shocked and angry at what happened to our car." Anna continued, as late afternoon threw the room into deepening shadows. She stood to clear the dishes, and turned on lights which reflected softly off the dark paneled walls.

"At first when it happened, Jus told me that the damage had been done by a student group while he was parked off Ku'dam. He said there was a demonstration. I thought it sounded far-fetched, but it was possible. There were demonstrations constantly: students marching with their street wide banners, chanting and sounding loud horns. But he wouldn't report it to the Politzei or MPs, and refused to file a claim for insurance.

"Meanwhile, debris of some sort had been piled in a corner of the garage, and there were signs of disturbance. The floor looked recently swept. You may think it unlikely, but I felt an aura of violence permeating the space. I later wondered if the car had been vandalized right there.

Anna looked over at her mother. "A few days later Mutti was able to get word to us of visits by the Stasi and others after Justin came to her house. Then, I became very suspicious and concerned, what with the ravaged car, the unknown men's questions, and Justin's nervous behavior. But he never conceded to me of any connection."

Anna's mother, who had been listening, nodded and shook her head, her blue eyes looking both sad and angry. In spite of her hardships and age, Louisa was still an elegant lady. Also alert and articulate. Louisa picked up the story in precise High German. "Justin always was a courteous and kind gentleman. At first, I was disappointed when Anna married an American, but Justin was from a good Bürger family." She paused, "And I changed my mind. He made many trips to me bringing items hard to acquire that enhanced my day-to-day life. He also brought medication and Deutsch marks. I knew Justin took great risk, because he didn't declare everything."

In a soft voice, Louisa continued, "Although in the early 70s it became possible for Anna to visit us in the East, it was easier for Justin to make more frequent visits. He crossed at the point where foreigners crossed, and wasn't scrutinized so closely." Feeling an emotional overload, Alexis wondered if she was ready for the rest of Louisa's story.

* * *

West Berlin: January 1988

Saturday morning, Justin went down to the garage. Whenever he thought about it years later, he still experienced every feeling and essence as if he were still living the event. He had errands to run and was on the way downtown. He wanted to work out at the health club and check on the bag.

When Justin entered the garage, he stood in shocked amazement. All four doors to the car were open. The floor was littered with the contents of the trunk and interior pockets. The floor mats were out as well, tossed in several directions Approaching the car, Justin saw that the seat cushions were pulled out and slashed, the glove compartment was broken open and partly dislodged. An open space in the floor told him the intruders had found the compartment. *My God.* He stood there for a minute paralyzed with fear. He looked around with alarm wondering if anyone was lurking in the garage. *What about outside?*

Until then, the week had passed without incident, although Justin was anxious and expectant. Nothing more was said at work about Peter's arrest and only a short mention appeared in the German press. Not that this meant that he was off the hook. He expected every day to be approached. He wasn't naïve. He knew Peter's connections wouldn't simply abandon the goods. Justin speculated how much the stuff might be worth. He supposed it was heroin, although that was a guess.

By Wednesday, Justin had his story if he was approached. It would be risky, and he knew how ruthless these people were, but he believed he could be convincing.

Instead, they seized the package during the night. Justin's fear was intense. He remembered how he felt in Viet Nam: crouched in the jungle, waiting for the unseen enemy stalking him. As he appraised the extent of damage to the car, he could sense the culprits' fierce anger. *Will they come for me next?*

* * *

"In the morning of the second day after Justin's visit, two men came to my house and forced me back from the door. The men looked in all the rooms; they made me sit, and asked me questions about Justin: 'Where does Justin live? Where does he work? When will he be back?'

"I didn't understand why they asked such questions; Justin's visits were well documented at the checkpoint. They were rude and threatening, and one made a point to let me see the gun under his coat. It didn't make sense, but they were frightening."

Anna got up to answer the phone. "Excuse me. Mutti, go on. I'll see who this is."

Louisa nodded. She appeared eager to tell her story. "When the men left, one grabbed my wrist and pulled me close to him. 'Don't tell anyone about our visit or we'll be back,' he said, and threw me back into my chair." She looked shaken just remembering the scene. "I didn't know what to do, and didn't leave the house all day. The following morning, the Stasi came, and I told them what happened." Alexis was riveted to the account.

Louisa took a breath. "It was then that I realized the other men were connected to something else, but I couldn't imagine why they were interested in Justin. It took me several days to get the news of the visits to Anna." Louisa fell silent; the memory obviously had taxed her. Alexis sat drained as well.

"That was Matthias. He'll arrive tomorrow. He's anxious to see you, Alexis, and eager to talk to you about Justin." Anna returned to the room.

"That's unexpected, how nice. Did you know?"

"He told me he was going to come if he could get away. I didn't say anything until I knew it was for certain. We'll call you at the hotel once he arrives. Do you have any special plans for tomorrow?"

"Nothing particular. Talking with Matthias will be an extra pleasure." Alexis stood, "Now, you really must let me go. Your mother looks tired, and I know you have plans for the evening. I'm drained myself. I need time to absorb everything. Would you call a taxi for me?"

"Of course. Mutti and I will look forward to seeing you again." Anna turned to make the call while Alexis shared parting words with Louisa.

A few minutes later, the sharp cold bit into her face as Alexis went out to the waiting cab. She had an eerie feeling as she prepared to get in. It was as though she were being watched. *The way Justin must have felt after he found the car!*

The cab skirted the Dahlem Museums and the Bontanischer Garten, now illuminated in the late afternoon darkness. *A lovely area to live in. Anna must have been gratified when she was able to claim the apartment, and then to raise her family here.* Alexis thought it ironic that Louisa was living out her last years in the apartment where her husband had kept a mistress. *When did she find out, or did she always know?*

As they drove closer to Ku' dam, she thought it may have been the route Justin often followed. The narrations she had heard that afternoon kept coming back in flashes and pieces. She shivered in the warm taxi.

Arriving at the hotel, Alexis decided to take a quick walk to clear her mind. She was pleased Matthias was coming. *He must be very concerned.* Now he would hear more details, and maybe add some insights of his own. *And maybe he'll have a chance to show me some of the new Berlin.* She went in to relax before dinner. *God, what a day!*

Chapter Nine

Alexis woke after eight. Bright sun and clear skies promised a frigid day. She ordered breakfast to her room, and turned on the TV for news. Still waiting for room service, Alexis checked her e-mail. She was eager for follow-up to the meeting Travis had with Mary. The message that was waiting came as a shock. The narrow escape by Travis from the attack at the boat works left her numb.

Everything Travis had encountered during his investigation in Toronto left little doubt that Peter was connected in some way with drug activity. Was this the link to Peter's contact with Justin? After all these years, why pursue him now? Was there confirmation anywhere that Peter had been involved with drug trafficking in Berlin, along with his other activities? Who was the man that recognized Justin in Dresden? *What do we know, and what do we think we know?*

Alexis reviewed Anna's narration once more. Justin made periodic trips to Louisa in East Berlin. At the same time Justin made his last trip, Peter was arrested by the German police. Two days later, Louisa was roughed up by unknown men asking about Justin, and they searched her apartment. Justin's car was vandalized in what might have been a search. That is, if his story claiming it was done by student demonstrators was discounted.

After pondering the matter for almost an hour, Alexis made a call to *Berlin Morgenpost*. "I'm here in Berlin researching some events that took place back in the nineteen eighties. Is it possible to gain access to microfiche and back editions in your library?" After giving more information about herself and her purpose, Alexis was told to call back the next morning. She may have to come and talk with Herr Jung.

Frustrated by the process, Alexis wondered if it was worth pursuing. Would she find coverage of Peter's arrest and trial? Would there be anything to suggest drug trafficking? With everything that went on in Berlin at the time, Alexis was hard pressed to convince herself the press would consider it newsworthy. *I'll give it a shot.*

* * *

West Berlin: February 1988

"Dad, I can't believe you're going to come with the team to Frankfurt on the troop train!" Philip and Matthias laughed uproariously. "You! You know how crowded and uncomfortable the bunks on the train are, not to mention the rooms in billeting where we'll stay." Philip whooped again.

"Yeah, and the guys are going to give us a really bad time, Dad. Why all of a sudden are you volunteering to chaperon?" Matthias, still laughing, threw himself into a chair, and covered his head in mock horror.

"I haven't done anything for the school while they put up with the two of you all this time, and Coach was happy to take me up on it." Justin returned their laughter. "So was the cheerleader sponsor. I think you two worry her the most. George Barrette's father is going as well, so you can share the humiliation with George." He stood up to leave the den.

"They're working on getting me the flag orders and adding my name to the travel roster. So get over it," Leaving the room, Justin laughed some more, and tousled Philip's hair. "And I'll get to see you both play. Naturally, I'm expecting a championship."

The Berlin American High School basketball team was going to the Triple A Division European Finals being held that year in Frankfurt. Sifting through his options, Justin had decided on a risky plan. He would try to deal the package through contacts he knew in Frankfurt who could make the necessary connections. He couldn't keep it here in Berlin, and he didn't know what or when to expect new action from Peter's associates. Anna was angry and suspicious with him about the car, and the investigation was heating up at work. Taking the package on the troop train was chancy, but within the cover of a group of high school players and cheerleaders, he thought he could slip it out.

The evening of departure, all went smoothly. Coach handled the passports and travel orders with the MPs, while the team, sponsors, and assistants were herded to their car and compartments. It was a familiar routine for Berlin teams as well as incoming opponents.

When he saw the dogs, Justin could feel the perspiration starting under his shirt and his scalp prickle. But their group was simply waved through. He threw his bags on a top bunk in the compartment for four, and breathed with relief. "Kind of tight quarters," he remarked lightly to another of the coaches, "but it's only for one night. Do the kids let us sleep, you think?" It would be an uncomfortable night, but it was perfect cover, and it would get the job done.

"We're lucky," one of the coaches said with a laugh, "these compartments usually make up for six."

* * *

Over lunch Matthias was regaling Alexis with his memory of the famous trip to Frankfurt when his father volunteered as a chaperon. The guys gave Justin a raucous time, the Berlin Bears beat Heidelberg to win the European basketball championship, and, Mathias speculated, Justin may have taken out a package of drugs.

Anna reluctantly agreed about the drugs. She said she was surprised and incredulous when Justin told her he was making the trip with the team. "I just couldn't believe it. It was so out of character for him. He liked to travel first-class only, and certainly wasn't interested in being involved with groups of teenagers for an extended time. With all that was going on at work, I thought he must have lost his senses. Yet just now listening to Matthias, it struck me that this was indeed the way he could smuggle something out of Berlin."

Alexis asked some questions about the military train carrying American troops and civilians across East Germany between West Berlin and Frankfurt. She also asked how much time Jus had away from the team during the tournament.

"Oh, he didn't have to stay much with us once we were playing. He watched our games and was billeted with the team, but he had plenty of time to look up friends. You know . . ." Matthias looked thoughtful, "He went back about a month later, but that time he flew."

"He went back to Frankfurt?"

"Yes," Anna added. "I remember. Justin said it was connected to an AAFES managerial meeting. Periodically, he did go out to meetings, and it didn't surprise me as it did when he chaperoned the team. I thought he might have been called out as part of the investigation. I think he used the trips to get over to Luxembourg."

"Luxembourg?" Alexis asked.

"Yes." Anna became more intense, her memory fully engaged, "You see, about a year before the incident, I came across some papers that were from a bank in Luxembourg. Justin said they handled some of his investments, and brushed it off as nothing special, but I'm sure it was a numbered account which neither the American nor German government knew about. That's how some Germans hide their money to avoid the high taxes. It's probably where Justin put the money he got from his dealings with Peter."

"A numbered account." One more piece fell into place. Alexis thought of the money trail Travis had tracked. "You don't remember the name of the bank by any chance?"

Anna shook her head. "I don't know. I'll have to think. It's been a long time."

"Of course. Don't worry over it too much, but it might be important if you can remember."

"Let me think about it." She said again. "What do you think about the return trip to Frankfurt?" Anna was eager to hear Alexis' reaction.

Alexis looked at Matthias. "It could be significant, but it's hard to say. If Jus did carry out drugs on the team trip, he may have made arrangements for someone to unload them there in Frankfurt. It would have been a dangerous venture, but by now, I'm ready to believe almost anything about your father. This all has been well beyond anything I expected to hear."

Alexis thought of Jackie, who didn't have a clue. She had a sick feeling, her lunch turned in her stomach. Anna and Louisa nodded sadly, and Matthias shielded his eyes with his hand shaking his head, "Oh, Dad. You dumb fuck."

* * *

Later in the day, Alexis and Matthias were strolling through the Zoo in the Tiergarten. The Central European winter air was brisk and invigorating, and helped dispel the subdued mood with which the lunch conversation had concluded. Alexis could tell that Matthias was troubled, and wanted to discuss topics away from his mother and grandmother.

"I'm so glad you suggested this. How did you guess? Of course, we must see the pandas!" Alexis laughed with genuine joy.

"I remember you telling Philip and me how much you liked zoos when we were skiing in Italy. We kidded you about it, and you gave us a finger."

Alexis laughed again, "You deserved it. You both were incorrigible."

"We were, but you didn't seem that much older, and we both had crushes on you. You made your point though. When I got back, I read Ryan's *The Last Battle*, including the story of the animals in the zoo. I talked about it so much that dad read it just to shut me up. This became one of my favorite places."

"I know you're very worried about your dad. I'm sorry if my visit has caused you disappointment." They were approaching the panda area.

"I'm worried, but I pretty well knew about most of what you've heard. Philip was in college in the States when my dad first went to Dallas. Mother stayed here so I could graduate. We went to Dallas for Christmas and Easter break. I missed the ski trips we used to take. Everything had changed. Then my grandfather died and left dad a big inheritance. He decided to leave AAFES and buy into his uncle's business. Mother refused to leave Berlin, but I think what Dad had been involved in finished it for her. She felt disappointed and betrayed."

A cluster of birds were flushed into flight, settling in the branches of bare trees. Two children appeared chasing one another. Matthias continued the family history. "Sometime after the divorce, she told Phillip and me most of the story. The part about transporting drugs is new and hard to take, but I think either Mother wasn't sure, or just wouldn't let herself acknowledge it. She says dad admitted the black marketing, but stuck to his story about the car in spite of what happened to Oma." They reached the entrance, and their attention shifted to the pandas.

For another hour or so they meandered to look at and speak to a few of their favorites, lions and elephants, and then stopped at a kiosk cafe for coffee. The zoo was on winter hours and would close at five. Matthias took up the previous topic.

"Do you think dad's involved with drugs there in D.C.?"

Alexis could tell Matthias dreaded asking the question. "I don't know for sure, but the way things developed, it doesn't seem to be that. We can't rule it out yet either."

"Can you tell me more about how they did develop? Why did Jackie ask you to become involved? Is he really in danger, or is this something to do with Jackie?"

Before she answered, Alexis poured coffee from the kenchen, and then asked her own question, "Do you think your father's marriage is a good one?"

Matthias didn't answer right away. He was thoughtful. "Yes." Then looking up he added, "But you know my dad. It's something I never could entirely understand. Even now.

"Growing up, I never thought much about his marriage to my mother. Everything taken into consideration we had a good life. My parents had many friends, German and American, and enjoyed one another. They were great parents. But it was as if dad constantly had to be revalidated as successful, glamorous, and virile. You saw how he was when we were skiing. There's something unfulfilled in him, and that's what drives him to risky and reckless actions. Not that I'm a perfect guy."

Alexis marveled at how insightful the young man sitting before her was about his father. "Would you prefer this be about Jackie and another woman, or that he's involved in drugs?"

The cafe was hot, overheated, common in German establishments. It was crowded in spite of being mid week, the windows steamed over. Winter was not the best time to visit the Tiergarten when it came time for coffee. In summer, they would be sitting at outside tables under the trees. In summer, they might be having wine or beer.

"Bones in the schrank."

"What?"

"Bones in the schrank." Matthias smiled, and his expression was of one who had resolved a dilemma. Alexis had a flash memory of the antique standing closet in the Lawrence home. Mathias eagerly continued, "I had a German friend whose mother married an American tech representative working here in Berlin. When Gerhard enrolled in our school he didn't speak much English, but he was very bright, worked hard, and learned quickly. I was fluent in German, and became a friend while helping him.

"You know," he continued, clearly enjoying himself, "slang and expressions are usually the hardest, and one day he had me rolling on the floor with laughter." Matthias set down his cup freeing his hand to gesture as he spoke. "We were talking about our families and parents, and he told me that, of course, every family had bones in the schrank. I asked, 'What are you talking about?' After some discussion I realized he was referring to the expression 'skeletons in the closet.' Bones in the schrank! It was hilarious. I didn't know if he was being clever, or trying a translation. It didn't matter. We both laughed until tears ran down our face."

Alexis was taken back by the change in tenor of their conversation. Matthias had become almost jovial in telling his story. She couldn't help but laugh. Two matrons at the next table looked over in disapproval.

"I guess that's an answer."

"Yes, it is." Matthias came back to the present. "You see, whatever's going on is something over which we really have no control. We can't redo what's happened, anymore than we can keep our lives and conditions the way they were. Dad seems to have a lot of bones in the schrank, some we don't know about, but so does everyone. Most of them, we hope, will never be uncovered while we get on with our lives."

"Or come out of the schrank?" They both laughed in spite of the looks. Returning to his earlier question, Alexis declared, "Matthias, I think your father is in danger."

Chapter Ten

"... I told you what happened. I'm really sorry. I lost the keys while down at the yacht club. You'll have to send someone down to pick it up." Travis repeated his explanation to the rental agent one more time trying not to sound exasperated.

"Why didn't you call us? We could have brought you some keys." The agent clearly was put out by what he thought was a glib explanation. "We'll have to add an extra charge for it all."

"I understand. I was late for an appointment and had a friend take me back to my hotel. Right now, I have a flight to catch. Can we settle this up?" Travis wondered what condition the car was in, and if Riffi had searched it to find leads to him. The rental contract carried both his name and North Carolina address.

"I cannot total your bill until we retrieve the car and assess any damage. There is also the cost for filling the tank. Wait here. I'll discuss this with my supervisor!" The agent stepped away from the counter and went into a small office. Travis fidgeted and checked his watch. He may just make the flight if the jerk agent would hurry.

Finally in the air, Travis set aside the problem over the car, and for much of trip he turned his thoughts to what he had learned about Peter, as well as the questions concerning Justin. Was Justin a player or prey? Where was Peter? Had they disappeared together? If a double-cross to an international gang was involved, Justin and Peter would be on their list for a long time.

Travis glanced out the small window: at this altitude the sky was cloud free and blue. Bright sun reflected off the wings of the 737. He returned to his thoughts. With all Justin had going for him, why would the man get mixed up in such a dangerous scam? Was he stupid, reckless, or both?

The connecting flight from Cincinnati arrived at Dulles in the early afternoon. With the rest of the passengers, Travis took a shuttle into the terminal and headed for baggage pickup. He looked around to note anyone that might be a new watcher waiting at this end. He was certain that Riffi found his rental agreement in the glove compartment of the car. Would they look for him in Carolina? Do they think he can lead them to Justin?

Before picking up his bag, Travis called the motel located within the terminal grounds and confirmed a room. Once outside Arrivals, he welcomed the mild afternoon temperature. Cars and buses pulled up and departed, a scene complicated by the throng of newly arrived travelers crossing the lanes. After a short wait the courtesy van arrived. He would operate from here for a few days. If he was being watched, there wasn't much they could learn from this location.

Travis checked in and changed into jeans and a hooded top. Relaxing on the bed, he made a phone call and arranged to be picked up by Pat, his operative monitoring the phone tap. A little after six, he was met at a side entrance.

"Thanks for coming."

"No problem. You think you're being followed?" They pulled away from the motel and headed for the airport exit.

"It's hard to say yet. It's possible, which is why I'm staying where I am. I doubt they could put all the pieces together in time to arrange for someone to meet my flight. Keep your eye out."

"Will do."

"You say we've had a contact? Where did the call come from?" Travis was eager to hear about the new development.

"St. Kitts. A bank. It was a little tricky tracing it back." Pat pumped his fist in triumph over the coup. "You'll be able to listen later. Want to eat first?"

Travis was excited. A breakthrough. "Might as well. We can talk over dinner and some more at your place. Airplane food is lousy and I didn't have breakfast. I tried to get out as early as I could but first had to clear up the little problem with the car rental."

"I want to hear more about your swim," Pat laughed. "I thought you'd given up that sort of recreation."

"So did I. Just drive." Travis was chagrined, but also could laugh. "This investigation has become very complicated."

They left the Dulles road at the 495 Beltway exit, and headed south. Rush hour traffic was still heavy, although so far there were no accidents, and they moved steadily. Pat's apartment was in Alexandria, and Travis assumed they would eat somewhere close. He kept an eye on the mirrors, but the reflecting headlights and traffic volume made it impossible to tell if they were being followed. He doubted anyone had noted his arrival, but he remembered Alexis telling him Jackie's story about the accident and that someone had been tracking Justin.

All in all, Travis decided, if they want to pick me up again it will be in Carolina. In the morning he would call the Captain alerting him to watch for strangers casing out the house. He wanted to talk with Alexis as well. It was time for her to come back, so they could plan the next moves. *St. Kitts. Not a bad choice for anonymous banking. Is Justin living holed up nearby? Is Peter with him?*

* * *

November: New York

Shortly after four in the afternoon, Justin left his room with towels on the bathroom floor and bed unmade as though slept in. He closed the door behind him and took the elevator to the parking garage. Two hours before he had settled the bill and alerted the motel for an early morning departure. Earlier in the day, Jus had called Peter at his motel near LaGuardia and told him he wasn't going to drive in for the money exchange.

"That isn't a good idea," Peter shouted. "I expected to meet here in the city. I don't know how the trains work. And how come you drove?" He sounded anxious and upset.

"It's easy. This way is better." Without giving Peter a chance to reply, he patiently explained what to do and said he'd pick him up outside the North White Plains station. "I'll start looking for you with the 5:02 arrival. Come out to the curb and I'll pull up for you. I know a great little restaurant where we'll—"

Peter interrupted. "I don't like it."

"—finalize the arrangement."

"I don't like it. What if I miss you? I want to meet here."

"You won't miss me. I'll wait until you get here if you don't make the first train. I don't want to bring my car into the city," he said again. "Cars don't last an hour sometimes."

"Oh, get off it, Justin. Put it in a parking garage. I don't know anything about those swanky suburbs. Why didn't you talk about it the other day when we made plans? And when did you decide to drive?" Peter was pissed.

Because I wanted to surprise you and any friends who may be along, "It'll be much better this way. Besides my car, I don't like carrying luggage through the streets. I didn't feel good about carrying it on a plane either," he kept on not allowing Peter a word. "You always handled that end, and it probably wouldn't faze you, but I'm very nervous over these arrangements. New York isn't Berlin, you know. It's better all around. How do you think the cash would look on the baggage security belt?"

"*Scheisse!*" Peter exclaimed.

"Don't be an *Esel.*"

"Fuck you! I tell you I don't like it. It stinks."

"Peter, I can't come in. You'll have to come out. Or we can reschedule for another way. Maybe I could drive out to Buffalo and meet you at the border."

"*Scheisse.*" Peter said again. "That's not possible. It's gotta be now. I've got to think. Give me your number." There was a mummer in the background.

While you discuss it with . . . ? Justin nodded to himself.

Thirty minutes later, Peter called back. "Okay. I still think it stinks, but I can make it work. Tell me about the trains again. Do they run the other way at night or do I have to stay out there?" He sounded as if he were going to a foreign country.

"You'll be able to get back to the city. I'll pick up a schedule for you while I wait." Justin repeated his instruction about the trains. "I'll see you a little after five. Buy a paper to read on the train. You'll fit right in."

"*Scheisse.*"

Justin smiled to himself with satisfaction. "Your vocabulary hasn't grown a bit," but the phone was dead. He paced the room to calm himself down. He hadn't lied when he told Peter he was nervous. His palms sweat as he thought about what was ahead. "I've got to do it." Justin said aloud.

*   *   *

The next morning, Travis mulled over the previous night's revelations as he finished his breakfast and third cup of coffee. The recorded call from St. Kitts was short and short on information. Justin asked question to assure him that everything was going well with Jackie and the children. He asked if Jackie had been approached or threatened. Louis told him there had been nothing as far as he knew. Justin said he was situated, but did not say where. "I'll be in touch if I need you."

After listening twice to the tape, Travis and Pat debated about how much Justin had revealed to his lawyer before disappearing. Yet this morning, Travis couldn't help feeling vindicated. It was now confirmed that Justin's disappearance had been planned, and he had not fled in panicked haste. In December, Travis had reasoned that if this were the case, the logical person to cover Justin and his affairs was his lawyer. And that's what proved out. Travis knew he would have to be careful with Alexis about this outcome. He suspected she was still angry about the arrangements he made with Pat without her consent.

Outside, the mild weather of yesterday had changed to a cold bitter day. Dark skies indicated approaching rain, sleet, or snow, depending on the temperature. Planes were still flying in and out with regularity, but that seemed certain to change as the day wore on. Streets were certain to become slick and messy. Travis shivered. He realized he hadn't gotten over his unexpected swim. Nursing the last bit of coffee, he gave himself a few minutes to confront once again the close call, and admit how close it had been. Now, he would put it behind him.

Travis signed the check to his room and left a tip. He thought again about urging Alexis to return from Berlin. The situation was changing rapidly. They needed to bring Pat in directly, but knew he needed approval for that, as well as to reveal her identity. Pat knew of his previous connection to Lucas, but not that Alexis had continued with the work. Travis had let him think he was connected to the special contractors operating out of Myock in North Carolina.

The situation was getting tricky. He was identified by Peter's colleagues, and soon Alexis would be as well if they pursued him to the Outer Banks. Travis passed through the lobby area and walked down a hall to his room. Closing the door, he sat down at the computer and waited for the connection. He then sent an e-mail to Alexis saying he had arrived back in D.C. and alluding to the taped call, he urged her to return ASAP without including give-away details to any potential hackers. Then he called Jackie.

"Mrs. Lawrence? This is Travis. I work with Alexis and was at your house in December. Remember?"

"Of course. Is there anything wrong? Where's Alexis?" Jackie was preparing to leave for the museum.

"Nothing's wrong. Alexis is still in Berlin. Have you heard anything new?" Travis pictured the tall slender woman on the other end, her long black hair pulled away from her face and held by a clasp at the nape of her neck. After his experience in Toronto and hearing the taped conversation, he had all but eliminated his suspicions of her.

"No. Nothing. Have you found out anything?" Jackie sounded stronger and less hesitant than when they last met. Hardly a month ago, Travis thought with surprise. *It seems like three.*

"Nothing to tell us where he is or what happened." Travis told a casual lie. "Have the phone calls stopped?"

"At least the ones at night. I'm not here all the time during the day. I have a housekeeper, but she hasn't mentioned anything."

Thinking of the call between Justin and Louis, Travis asked, "Did you tell anyone besides Phillip and Alexis about the threatening calls?"

"Why no. I don't think so. Should I?"

Ignoring the question Travis replied, "I'm back here in Washington and would like to come over again and check some more things in your husband's office. Would this be possible?"

Jackie paused. What did Travis think he missed? "When do you want to come? I'll be out until about three. Margaret will be here though."

"I'd like to come when you're there. Would 3:30 be okay?" He wished it could be sooner.

"That'll work. Would you like to stay for dinner? I'll be sure there's enough, if you're not too choosy. I'm not sure what we've planned for tonight."

"That's very kind of you, Mrs. Lawrence. Can we play it by ear? I don't know how much time it will take, but I may not be long at all."

"That'll be fine. Have you heard from Alexis?"

"A few bits and pieces. Nothing specific," Travis fudged. "She's met with Anna and her mother, but I don't know what she's found out. I think she's making herself something of a tourist as well, but don't let her know I said so."

Jackie laughed. "It sounds like Alexis. I'm hoping her trip will be helpful."

"Me too. I'll see you later today."

Travis was eager to reexamine the home office. He had noticed some e-mails on Justin's computer in December that in hindsight could be important, but at the time he was tracing other information, and didn't give them much attention. Now, it may provide a new piece of the Justin Lawrence puzzle.

By 3:30 the weather rapidly was turning worse. The roads were slick with rain mixed with snow. Using Pat's 4 X 4, Travis negotiated the neighborhood streets in McLean and parked in the Lawrence drive. Margaret met Travis at the door. "Mrs. Lawrence is upstairs with her children. She will be down shortly. She said I should take you to the study."

Travis took of his coat and left it in the hallway next to what he recognized as an antique German schrank. He followed the nanny to the study, sat at Justin's desk, and turned on the computer. He quickly immersed himself in Justin's e-mail.

Travis scanned the lists of incoming and outgoing messages. He opened a few. He found matches for some "Sent" and "In". Justin had been in contact with two web sites that offered software to create a wide array of identification documents. *Did he download or buy? Where's the software?*

"Good afternoon. Are you finding anything new of value?" Jackie came into the study.

"Mrs. Lawrence, good afternoon." Travis stood to greet her. He preferred she not look too closely at the screen.

"I fixed some hot cider for the children and brought you a mug. It's turned nasty outside. Burr."

"That sounds great. Thank you." Travis looked closely at Jackie as she handed him the cup and a plate of ginger snaps. She didn't appear as drawn and nervous as she had in December. He noted again how attractive she was, but now she looked resolute.

"Do you use this computer for your work?"

"Not often. I have my own in the den upstairs. Of course, I use the network at the gallery." She sat in one of the chairs to chat while Travis meandered around the room studying the case containing the gun collection and rifles. Next to it were shelves of books.

"I came back to check some things I didn't look at very closely in December. I'll probably go through some of his software again. Do you know if Jus kept any elsewhere in the house?" Travis pulled out a book on handguns, and noticed a few others including two on rifles and one on swords and armor. From the books Jus didn't appear to have interest in assault weapons and other military devices.

"I don't think so. He was very exact about where he kept his records and communications. You've seen how he keeps the accounts and checkbooks." Jackie paused to consider the possibilities. There's a safe in the house, but I don't know why he'd put something like that in there. Would you like for me to look?" Jackie filled her mug from the pitcher on the tray. Travis turned from the books after noticing the worn collection of Hemingway, a couple of Robert Ruark and other authors he didn't recognize. Most of Justin's collection revealed a personal collection of genuine interest.

"I don't think so right now. Let's see what I find." He had a sudden thought. "What you can do is provide me with a couple of pictures of your husband. We might use them when we ask if he's been seen."

"That won't be difficult. Is there anything else you need?"

Travis turned once more to the gun collection. He noted there was an empty mount which caused the display to appear unbalanced. A slight difference in shading revealed where a gun had been placed for awhile allowing the surrounding area to fade. "I wonder if you can tell me anything about this gun collection. I notice some very valuable pieces."

"That's right. Justin said that several were collector items. I don't know much about them except that most were obtained during his years overseas. He did say there was a very complex procedure to bring them back. That was a few years before we married, so I don't know what was involved. The case is locked and has a security alarm. Only Jus has a key and knows how to disarm it."

"Do you know if he ever uses any? Like in target practice or such." Travis looked more closely to note their condition. All appeared well maintained.

"Jackie frowned, "I don't know for sure. I don't think so, except his hunting rifles. Jus belongs to a shooting club, but he keeps his guns for that out at the range." She considered the question, "But I guess he could take one over on occasion. We seldom discuss his shooting. We just agreed that there would be no guns in the house that were not locked up."

Jackie left her chair and walked over to look at the collection with Travis. She didn't seem to notice anything out of order, but her casual appraisal suggested she didn't know much about the pieces anyway. Travis decided she had nothing to hide, and nothing more to tell him. Yet his instincts told him that Justin left for New York with more than his Purdey. *If so, why did Jus take a pistol from his collection, and not one from the club? Interesting. Alarming.*

"But I'm keeping you from your work." Jackie refilled a mug leaving it on the table. "I'll go look for some pictures. Do you think you'll be staying for supper?"

"Let me see how the search goes. It's still early, and the streets are getting worse. If I can finish up here in the next hour, I think I'd better get back to the motel." Travis looked at her and smiled. "I really appreciate the cider and cookies though. Haven't had any since I went off to college. My mom used to fix it for me and my sister when we'd come in from sledding."

After Jackie left the room, Travis sat down again at Justin's desk. Twenty minutes later, he hit pay dirt. Mixed in with accounting CDs and a copy of "Myst" was one with the inconspicuous title "Documents." He almost passed it up as another record keeper, but thinking of the e-mail review, he put it in the CD drive to play. A quick perusal satisfied him it was important. He closed the disk and put it into his leather case. The next half hour was spent searching Justin's files for identity documents.

Travis looked out the window and could see that the storm was becoming more intense. He'd like to stay longer; there might be more of value to discover. With a sigh he shut down the computer. *Better go. Still, it would be nice to know what Justin is calling himself these days.*

* * *

November: The Adirondacks

The cabin was dark and unoccupied, just as he expected. Justin didn't think Martin let many people use the place without him being there. Through the woods, a small distance away though, faint light was visible from another camp. Not surprising, considering the season, but he knew he'd have to work quietly. He'd be quick and show a minimum of light, but he had come to the cabin to get his bearings.

Using fog lights, Justin backed around carefully, headed out again to the road, and after a short distance spied the overgrown dirt road that cut off in the direction of the lake. He drove about a hundred yards. A shielded flashlight in hand, he got the tools from the back and walked off the road until he found a spot that satisfied him.

Justin worked mainly by the light of the three-quarter moon pulling, cutting away under brush, and then breaking ground with his pick and shovel. It was hard work, although the ground wasn't yet winter frozen, but he wanted to leave behind as little disturbance as possible. He filled a large leaf bag with cuttings and debris. The brush would grow back in the spring.

Before long he was drenched in sweat under his hunting jacket and pants, and he was panting from exertion. Although he worked out regularly at the health club, Justin's body was unaccustomed to the manual labor, and he still hurt from the accident on the Parkway. He felt his hands begin to sting beneath his gloves as they rubbed red and started blisters. Yet the activity also felt good, and he worked away his tension and anger at the circumstances that brought him here. As he caught his breath in the fresh cold air, he admitted to himself another feeling: regret.

Hunting always had been a sport for Justin and his brother. They had been introduced to it early by their father, and they looked forward to every fall season. Jus never gave much thought to the idea that stalking game reflected satisfaction in killing. But it was the army that taught him to kill people. He had flunked out of college after two years and enlisted before he was drafted. And all before his father learned of his failure. He knew he was never quite forgiven, and only partly redeemed by going to war.

Justin acknowledged to his closest friends he had not been an enthusiastic soldier, but once in the Viet Nam jungle, he used his training to survive. He remembered his first fire fight when a couple of the squad froze with fear and were unable to use their rifles. They died quickly; he survived. Later, looking back, Justin realized the whole time he was in Nam, he had harbored an unspoken thought that he was the prey, not his enemy. This bothered him, and years later he hunted with a different perspective.

Catching his former colleague unaware, and shooting him in the seat next to him had not been easy. It smacked almost as a cowardly act. Then again, when Justin braked unexpectedly, the silenced pistol had been steady. Using his left hand he fired across his chest as Peter jerked forward in his seatbelt. Not bad for a right hander.

Pausing again for breath in the woods, Justin thought how he had practiced the move along an infrequently traveled road near the Potomac River days before he departed for the rendezvous with Peter. Elation had not lasted long. When Justin pulled Peter upright in the seat, he smelled the blood. He gagged. Vomit covered his parka and jeans.

* * *

As soon as he got back to the motel, Travis put in a long distance call to Berlin. It was after midnight Berlin time, but Alexis was quick to answer.

"It's Travis. Did I wake you?"

"Actually, no, I got in a few minutes ago. Matthias took Anna and me out on the town." She laughed knowing how Travis would react.

"I should have guessed. Have you found out anything useful? I think you should come back. Did you get my e-mail?"

"The one I just read saying 'ET, come home'? You said there's been a contact."

"That, and now more, since I went over Justin's records again at their home. I think we need to regroup and move ahead. When do you think you can get back?"

Alexis thought a moment about the most reasonable timing. "Is there something urgent you've turned up? I'm going to one of the newspapers tomorrow to look through back issues."

"The call came from the Caribbean. I think we need to include Pat and send him down to look around while we go back to the Banks. No one knows about him, and they do about me. We don't want to lead anyone to Jus by accident. I want you to decide and let Pat know you're involved. If you agree, we should put together what we have so far and plan the next move."

Alexis quickly processed the information, "I probably can fly out to Frankfurt tomorrow and catch a return flight. I'll have to check. I've got an open ticket. That's if there is a seat. It shouldn't be too much a problem this time of year. At best, I'd arrive in the afternoon Thursday."

"That sounds good. It's not urgent, but I think we need to move. You'll know what I mean once we talk."

Alexis was eager to hear about the contact, but didn't push Travis for more details. *Justin's gone into hiding in the Caribbean. Not too surprising. What about Peter? Is he down there also, or somewhere else?* She put it out of her head, and went to bed exhausted.

Back at the motel, Travis sat back on the bed sipping a beer. He wasn't ready for supper and was musing over what he had learned at Jackie's house and throughout the last few days. Outside, the storm was whipping up.

What about Justin? With what kind of man were they dealing? Travis was concerned that Justin might have armed himself with a hard to identify weapon. If he was threatened by Peter and felt he needed to be armed, why not take the practice weapon with which he was familiar? And what was Justin's purpose in going to New York if he had decided to disappear?

At the same time Justin left for his hunting trip, Mary said Peter made a second trip to meet with Justin. Why? Were Justin and Peter meeting to exchange money, and then Justin planned to disappear?

The room seemed cold. Travis moved to the register and turned up the heat. Outside, the storm was raging. He opened the curtains and dimmed the lights to better watch the swirling snow.

Peter didn't return to Toronto. Did he take off with the money? But why did Justin need a gun? If the two had worked out a deal, then why did he need a gun? Was Peter armed? Did others go to New York with him? The thoughts tumbled over one another.

Travis shifted while watching the storm, thoughts racing. What was the leverage the group had on Justin? Where did Peter fit into the situation? What had Alexis found out about Justin and his connection to Peter? *Did Justin kill Peter?*

Travis started at the thought he had been suppressing. Wind was blasting snow in the parking area and the field beyond. The airport was shut down. All movement had stopped on the ground except for the buses carrying stranded passengers to nearby motels, and a few cars with last arrivals escaping to the suburbs.

Travis felt uneasy and restless. *Is my imagination carrying me away? Hurry up, Alexis. We've got much to discuss and plan.*

Meanwhile, in Berlin and Dresden a bitter cold front descended from Arctic Russia, Toronto was in the grip of a deep freeze, and in the Adirondacks heavy snow fell and drifted on the mountains and lakes.

* * *

Two days later, Alexis and Travis sat in a quiet corner of the lounge in the motel. Alexis had showered and relaxed for a couple of hours after arriving. Snow remained on the ground, and it was below freezing. The roads were mostly cleared, although patches of ice remained.

Alexis gestured to a window, "Some greeting. Washington isn't supposed to have this kind of weather."

"Oh, come on. You know they get at least one good storm a winter. Wasn't it cold in Berlin?" On a low table between them, Travis laid out printouts and other material he had gathered at Justin's computer.

"Yes, but it's supposed to be cold in Berlin. No snow or ice in the streets though." Although feeling jet lag, Alexis was eager to hear from Travis.

First, he briefed her on the identity program. They discussed it and then Travis drew her attention to the missing gun. "You know him. What is your take on Justin carrying a weapon?" He paused and added, "And why a piece from his collection rather than the one he uses to practice?"

Alexis didn't answer right away. She continued going through the documents in front of her while considering the questions. The information was disturbing, and she tried to fit it with the man she had known, first in Europe and later in Washington. "Until I saw the gun case in his home, I had no idea he was a collector. Lucas never mentioned it. We knew he went hunting: wild boar in Germany, and deer, I think, in the Adirondacks."

After a pause Alexis continued, "When I first talked with Anna the other day, I hadn't thought of Justin as much more than a superficial, self-centered person who enjoyed lavish living. That he might be involved in serious criminal enterprise never occurred to me. Even now, I can't quite see him exposing his precious self that way." She added, "Except possibly for the money. He definitely loves the money."

"If he enjoyed hunting and practiced with his pistol, he must have the wherewithal to use one if he felt he needed to." Travis leaned back in the chair and asked the question he had been waiting to ask. "Do you think Justin could have killed Peter?"

Startled, Alexis sat back from the documents in front of her. "Why do you think that? How could Peter be such a threat to Justin? It's the men that are using Peter to get to Justin who are the dangerous ones. Nothing we know or have heard about Peter suggests he is violent or even carried weapons." She drew a deep breath, "And whatever else Justin may be, I can't see him as a killer."

Travis leaned toward her and said almost in a whisper, "Maybe not. But if he were threatened or driven enough, he may decide it was necessary."

Alexis shook her head. "I can't imagine it." Suddenly she felt badly jet lagged: weary and light headed. "I don't think I'm ready to deal with all this right now. It's become far more complicated than I believed it could."

"I agree. It's become very complicated." Travis could see Alexis fading. "But before we break, I think you need to carry the scenario a few steps further." Not giving Alexis a chance to object, he continued. "Given the situation as it stands now, even if we locate Justin, you won't be able to reveal it to anyone, not even Jackie."

"What do you mean? Why?"

Travis pressed on. "Because they will continue to look for him. Or, if we locate Justin, but not Peter, we may have to somehow convince Makhmud and company that Peter is good for the money. Otherwise, they will continue to look for them both."

Travis glanced at Alexis to see if she was listening. "Okay, say Justin didn't kill Peter. Maybe Peter did take the money. When Justin realized it, he decided he had to disappear, although the planning he made doesn't support this picture."

Travis stopped to take a deep breath. Alexis looked at him in amazement.

Chapter Eleven

Hunched against the wind under a dreary sky, he was talking to Toronto. "The guy's not here, but I've found out a few facts about him. He's not a Fed. He's been out of the navy a few years and hangs out with the surfer crowd. Does some work for a company here that puts in security systems." Late Friday afternoon the jacket clad man was calling, back to the wind, from a pay phone outside a convenience store on Virginia Dare Trail. He had arrived on Wednesday, much to his disgust.

"He's not here. I told you that. It took me a while to find someone who even knows who he is, and that was luck. Asked for him in a local hangout; it turns out he sometimes works the bar. The whole place is pretty dead right now. Not many people. It's mostly a fucking beach resort. Nothing like Miami though. Asking around makes you look suspicious, so I have to be careful." JP was exasperated. They sent him because he'd fit in, and he shouldn't draw much attention. Only in the winter on the Outer Banks, the drifters and surfers had mostly moved out, and almost anyone new was noticed.

"I'll keep my eye out, but the house is way back from the road, in a sparsely populated neighborhood. Lots of houses are empty this time of year. The front's on the ocean. It's hard to get close enough to see much." He listened to additional orders.

"Right. I'll check in every couple of days." JP hung up cursing. He may look the part, but he'd rather be in Miami, not this cold half-deserted place. He decided to drive up to Norfolk for the weekend.

Travis had been back only a day when he dropped by The Safe Port to see what was happening, and who was around. The night before, few regulars were at Keoni's, but today was the first Sunday in February, so he wasn't surprised. Maybe George was around. His place was still open and popular for brunch.

"Look who dragged in! Where've you been? Want to work the bar any this week?" George was acting host for the patrons beginning to show up after church.

"How're things? I've been up to D.C., and I'm having a hard time finding anyone around. Came by to hear the latest.

"Sure, I probably can work tomorrow and Tuesday. I'll have to see after that. You usually don't need me this time of year."

"But Ralph's wife is just out of the hospital, and he has to watch the young ones. Little going on. A few more people closed up and are off for their vacation. We're closing for a month at the end of the week, but I need someone on bar until then.

"A guy asked about you last week. I didn't catch his name. Blond guy. He said you weren't at your place."

"Really?" Travis was sharply interested. "Did he say how he knew me? Give a name?"

"Don't know. He only talked to me a little. Two other guys here who knew you. He finished his beer talking with them. Haven't seen him since."

"You remember who the guys were?"

"Not really. I didn't pay them much attention. I can think about it."

"That's fine. What time you want me tomorrow?"

"If you could get here by five, it would help. Maybe only three or four hours. Monday's are slow."

"Sounds okay. I'll let you know if anything changes. See you then."

Travis was not surprised at what he had heard, only that it happened so quickly. Apparently the Toronto crowd was pursuing anyone that might help them find Justin and Peter. Or maybe more. *Don't forget they tried to kill you.* He hurried back to the house to call Alexis.

* * *

Travis was back in Kitty Hawk while Pat prepared to leave for St. Kitts to locate Justin. The morning following her arrival from Berlin, Alexis, Travis, and Pat met and resolved the touchy issues about whose investigation they were conducting. Sorting over the various options for controlling the challenges and dangers that had developed, the three agreed on a plan of action. What to do about Peter was left unresolved. Now, a day later and staying at a downtown hotel, she was steeling herself for a meeting with Jackie.

Over lunch which Alexis had ordered to the room, they spent a while discussing how Jackie was coping. Alexis was impressed by the improved demeanor reflected in Jackie's face and presence. *I underestimated her.* Alexis reflected thinking back to the carefree art history student studying in Florence when they first met. *Never prejudge.* Alexis wondered how much she was being prejudged as she worked through her loss of Lucas.

Jackie took the initiative. "Have you found out anything? Almost three months have passed without a word or trace."

Alexis was expecting the question. The task before her was delicate. How much to reveal, how much to withhold?

"We've made some progress. That's the main reason I wanted to talk with you."

"You found him?" Jackie looked both hopeful and fearful.

"No, not that." Alexis had decided she wouldn't talk about St. Kitts, the phone tap, or Louis' involvement. It was premature, and some of it she would never reveal. "We've reconstructed much of Justin's past involvement with Peter, which might tell us what brought him back into your lives. We've also tracked Peter back to Toronto," Alexis hesitated and then frankly stated, "only to find out that he also has disappeared. He was to meet Justin a second time in New York in November, and didn't return." She watched closely for Jackie's reaction.

Jackie looked hard at Alexis, narrowed her eyes in a frown, and slightly shook her head. "I'm not sure what you're saying. You think Justin went to New York to meet again with Peter and told me he was going hunting? Why? For what? Why would he lie to me, and why didn't he come home?" She looked genuinely concerned, while showing a spark of anger.

"We, Travis and I, don't have answers for everything. Much, so far, is only guess based on what we do know. This is difficult for you to absorb. I'm sorry. I need for us to go over what we have uncovered, and then you'll decide what you want me to do next." It was out on the table. Alexis waited for Jackie's reaction.

"I don't know what to say. Do you know if he's alive?"

Alexis lied, "We don't know either way for sure. There's nothing so far to indicate he's not." She gave Jackie the good news indirectly.

"Do you think Louis knows anything?"

Alexis showed nothing in her face at the question, but felt a lurch in her stomach. "I haven't had any contact with Louis. Why do you ask that?"

"Because he's been so reassuring. Because there's a power of attorney I didn't know about. Because he discouraged me from going to private parties to look into the situation. I have to be patient, he told me"

"I can try to talk with him if you want. Of course, it will mean his knowing you've gone against his advice and counsel." Alexis didn't want to confront Louis, but she was interested in Jackie's insight and reactions.

Jackie looked steely eyed at Alexis, another persona facet being revealed. "No, I don't think so. If he knows anything, he won't tell you. Lawyer-client privilege, he'd say."

Alexis was relieved; this would be a more helpful client than one who fell apart in despair and helplessness. "I think you're right," she said acknowledging the incisive conclusion. Alexis stood up. "Why don't we take a little break for a few minutes? I'll order some dessert and coffee. We can get back to it after we freshen up." And loosen up, she thought. The tension was taxing. There still was much to discuss.

Room service would take about thirty minutes. Alexis suggested a short walk outside in the cold. "We can do once around the block. It'll refresh us."

* * *

November: New York

Justin drove a short distance on the dark, deserted road away from the cabin towards Chestertown. At a shallow pullover, he stopped to take off the muddy jacket, pants, and boots, stuffed them along with the gloves and cap into large garbage bags, leaving him in jeans and a heavy pullover. Underway again, in spite of his exertion, and the heater going full blast, he couldn't stop shaking. He wondered if it was shock, or even the onset of hypothermia.

He drove to Lake George and found a motel where he checked in. "I had a late start from Montreal and had to stop." The night clerk shrugged, eager to get back to TV. Justin registered under a false name and paid cash. It was almost 3 a.m.

Once inside, he turned up the heat and poured a drink from his flask. The room was chilly, and Justin still was very cold. He took a long hot shower, wrapped himself in his robe, and draped himself with a blanket. Only then did he take apart and clean his gun, putting it away carefully in a small case. He thought briefly of going out for a snack, but wasn't hungry. Another drink in hand, Jus turned on the TV and flipped through the channels. Finding nothing he wanted to watch, he crawled into the bed and quickly went to sleep.

Justin slept until a little after eight. He felt like shit. Every muscle in his body ached, and his head felt worse. Dragging himself up, he took another hot shower. More awake and feeling slight improved, he shaved and dressed for the city in slacks, shirt, and a pull over sweater. A cashmere blend top coat was flung carelessly over a chair. The drive ahead was about five hours, and there were tasks to take care of before. He had to eat; he was weak with hunger and craved several cups of strong coffee. Guilty of murder, Justin glanced again in the mirror. *The first day of the rest of my life.* As though viewing a stranger, he studied the image. The reflection stared back in silence.

After a hearty breakfast at a nearby restaurant, Justin felt more himself. He was stiff, but his head no longer ached, and he was energized. First things first, then to the city. He had a train to catch that evening.

Instead of taking I-87, Jus took a local road to Glenn Falls. The first shopping center he cruised didn't have what he wanted, but the second one did. He drove to the service area at the back of one of the mall super mart stores, and stopped at a dumpster.

The area was clear of workers and delivery trucks. He quickly lifted the back hatch, pulled out the garbage bags of clothes and muddy boots, and threw them in the bin. He drove a few dumpsters down, stopped once more, and disposed of the work tools and debris. Satisfied with his work, he retraced his journey towards Lake George until he cut off to link up with an entrance to I-87. Justin headed south for New York. He began to think his plan would work.

* * *

Alexis and Jackie passed through the lobby and out into the bitter cold. The sidewalks and streets were clear, although remnants of ice and snow covered the curbsides. Little city traffic was out at the hour, and on Saturday it would remain that way. The two walked briskly for about fifteen minutes with hardly a word between them, each lost in their own thoughts.

Back once more in the warm hotel, they looked eagerly at the dessert and coffee. Settling back, Alexis picked up the initiative. "Can you tell me more about the hunting trip Justin was planning? I understood it had been canceled because Martin would be in London, and that you and Martha declined to go to keep Justin and Ron company."

Jackie looked surprised. She hadn't thought much about the change in plan when Justin proposed it. "I don't exactly remember." She paused to think. "You see, it was only about two weeks after our accident. Neither of us was seriously injured, although I had been shocked and frightened. Justin told the police he thought it was a hit and run, and I didn't remember then about his comments in the car I mentioned to you when we met in December. At times he was preoccupied in the days afterward, and busy at work, but there were no more calls and no more mention of Peter." Jackie took a bite of cake and sipped her coffee. She was thinking, but Alexis detected nothing to suggest deception.

"Sometime during the weekend, Jus said that he had just heard from Ron, who decided he wanted to go hunting after all, even though Martin wouldn't be with them. Jus asked if I minded if he went, was I feeling okay, that he thought it would be good for him, and so on. It wasn't something which particularly alarmed or surprised me."

Alexis was interested at Justin's approach. He must have counted on Jackie's sympathy for agreeing so easily.

"So you agreed?"

"I had no reason not to, and I knew he'd been under a strain. He'd been very concerned about me, and I wanted to reassure him I was okay, and not worried to have him go off. As I said, we had all but dropped the events before the accident.

"He was to leave Wednesday and try to return by late Sunday night, or stay over somewhere on the way back and come in Monday. I told him that was fine, just be home by Wednesday in time for Thanksgiving. I remember him laughing and saying not to worry because Ron had to go back to work."

"Do you remember if he did anything particularly unusual about getting ready to go?"

"What do you mean? I never paid much attention to his preparations. He packed his clothes and other items. Ron usually has food for the trips ready to take, or the guys get it on the way. And the camp is well stocked.

"It wasn't until later that I thought he must have taken his topcoat and some clothes he usually wouldn't need for a few days in the woods. Slacks and shirts, for instance, but I didn't think about it again; so much went on, and I was so upset."

"Have you looked over his clothes again? Did you find the coat?"

Jackie looked at Alexis again with questions. "No, not really. Why would I? It's hard for me to see his clothes in the closets and drawers, and think of him gone. His lap top's not here, but he'd probably take that even hunting, so I don't think it's unusual."

"One more question, I know this is hard. Were you aware at the time or did you notice since that Justin withdrew five hundred thousand dollars in cash from his personal bank account just before his last trip?"

"No!" she stated. "I don't look at his personal accounts."

"And you have no large sums of money in the safe in the house?"

Jackie nodded her head no.

* * *

November: New York

Jus reached the city by late afternoon. Rush hour had begun. A bad time to drive in New York, but good cover as well. When he first saw the sky line on his approach, he had a feeling of sadness wondering when, if ever, he would see his city again. He thought of his parents. This was not what they would have wanted for him.

Driving to a section of the Bronx chosen in advance, Justin began to look for a place to park. He needed a spot that was near a subway station since few cabs ventured into the area. It was not a great place for him to be, but for his plan to work, it was the place for his van. Trucks were double parked, and the traffic typically a mess. Horns blared, and people shouted from their cars.

After several minutes spent cruising the area, Justin pulled up at the end of a loading zone, and lapped over into the space occupied by a ConEd repair truck. He was ready to leave the van as a good enough job when the ConEd guys came out of a store.

"What the fuck you think you're doing? You've boxed us in!"

Jus got back in, gave them plenty of room to leave, and pulled back into the space. Another driver shook his fist at Justin, and leaned on his horn indicating he was going to take the spot. *Tough.* Justin refrained from using a hand gesture. This was not the time to get into an altercation.

Everything he wanted out of the glove compartment already was stuffed in one of his bags. Justin took out his luggage, and dutifully locked all the doors. Without looking back, he walked with purpose toward the subway. One bag he carried was packed with five hundred thousand dollars.

The sidewalk was uneven and crowded. Justin felt vulnerable and exposed. After descending the stairs, getting onto the subway car was awkward with all the people shoving through the doors against his bags. He would have to make a change after a few stops or try for a taxi closer in. Once underway, Jus relaxed a little, but he would stay vigilant until he was on the train.

* * *

Alexis sympathized with Jackie. She understood what she meant about the clothes; she experienced the same feelings when Lucas died. The matter of the cash withdrawal obviously was a shock. "Jackie, let me tell you some of the things we've learned about Justin and Peter. Some of it you may know, some of it will be difficult for you to hear. After I'm finished, I'll give you time to process it before you decide if you want me to continue looking for Justin."

Jackie nodded and Alexis began her narrative report explaining some, but not all of the possibilities she and Travis had put together. She intended to leave out the attack on Travis, the phone tap on Louis, as well as the missing gun from the collection and what that could suggest.

Jackie listened attentively. When the black marketing was mentioned, she nodded as if she were aware of the possibility. She broke in. "Justin told me about the charges and investigation, but he said he was exonerated."

"That's true, at least officially. I know it's painful to hear, but Anna says that Justin admitted stealing and black marketing. He got off, she says, because he covered his tracks more successfully than others who were implicated and convicted. What he didn't admit to was the connection to drug transport through Checkpoint Charlie, which is a great deal more serious, and the root of our situation today. That is, if we're correct. We don't have undisputed confirmation, but everything we know points to its reality."

Jackie started to protest, but shut her mouth. "I guess you'd better go on,"

Alexis continued with the Berlin story she put together on her visit. Jackie had paled, and become somewhat withdrawn. Alexis thought she might be tuning her out.

"I know you're shocked and may not want to believe it all. It's a lot to absorb. Do you want me to go on?"

Jackie took a deep breath. "I've got to hear it all before I say anything. Will you excuse me for a minute? I need to go to the restroom. I'll be right back." Alexis stood to stretch and walk around. She breathed deeply to relieve the tension. When Jackie returned, it appeared she had splashed water on her face messing her mascara. Her eye lashes were wet, yet she looked revived.

Alexis moved the venue to the U.S. and Canada speculating, as had Jackie, that the events of all the past three or four months were a result of the unexpected meeting in Dresden with someone from Justin's Berlin past. She explained how they traced the calls to Toronto, Travis' visit, and what he had learned. Alexis suggested that possibly Peter was extorting money from Justin, using the knowledge of the missing drugs and the previously suspected black marketing.

"So we've concluded that Justin decided at some point after the accident that to get away from the demand for money and draw the threat away from you and the children, he would go into hiding. We perceive a real danger to Justin, and finding him could expose him to this danger."

Alexis judged Jackie's appearance to be somewhere between absolute disbelief and absolute denial. A prolonged silence stretched into minutes while Jackie absorbed it all and considered her next statement. Waiting patiently for a response, Alexis thought she perceived anger replacing some of Jackie's other emotions. Was it at her for bringing the news, or at Justin who was its source?

* * *

November: New York

It took about thirty minutes for Justin to reach Penn Station. His train left at 7:05. He had time to spare. The reservations and tickets he paid for with cash in D.C. were inside his jacket pocket. These he had picked up at Union Station using his new identity.

Thinking of the long ride ahead, Jus bought sandwiches and snacks along with other items for the trip. He planned to use the dining car, but wanted to stay low profile. It would take twenty-seven hours to reach Miami. He had thought about getting off at Jacksonville and flying down and then decided the longer trip was an advantage. More time disappearing.

He would arrive close to ten in Miami and start work on a passport the next day. His nephew there once told him how easy it was: you make your connection in one of the hotels or places used by travelers from Central and South America. Sometimes drug and arms traffickers. Sometimes illegals. He already had an area picked out to start. Justin remembered the hot traffic stolen and false passports had been in Berlin, and the briefings he'd endured. He was sure he could handle it.

Carter Richards was able to board a half hour before departure. He closed the door to his compartment and unpacked. He poured himself a drink and sat back to relax for the first time since leaving his home only three days before. The train pulled out on time. By then Carter concluded his car had been stolen and was in a garage somewhere being prepped for a new paint job. He hoped they cleaned the upholstery on the passenger seat in the front.

* * *

"I'm not prepared to respond to this. I'm not prepared to believe that Justin is a criminal and someone who has or had dealings with drug trafficking. It's just not the Justin I know. I could not be that deceived." Jackie finally responded.

"I understand your feelings. I knew it would be difficult to hear, comprehend, and accept. I'm sorry, genuinely sorry."

"But you don't know for sure, do you? You said you were speculating, at least about the last part."

"That's right. I've given you the best explanation we can come up with so far. I can understand if you reject it. Given that, it's up to you to decide if you want me to continue trying to find Justin, or you want me to stop and you seek other avenues, or just wait for him to get in touch."

Jackie didn't respond right away. She sat back in her chair, head thrown back, eyes closed. She leaned forward looking at Alexis, "Incredible. Just incredible. Why would he leave that way without letting me know? How much more is there I don't know about him if it's true? I've had no reason to think he is anything other than what he's been." She was angry, Alexis knew, but tears were beginning to well.

Alexis reached across the table and put her hand on Jackie's arm. "There're still many unknowns. Justin may have made some bad mistakes in the past for which he hasn't answered, but maybe hoped he'd put behind him."

"You say he withdrew money out of the bank in cash? How much? You think Peter was blackmailing him somehow?"

"It's one possibility. Five hundred thousand. We think Peter was the contact, not the instigator. The money came out of the New York account, which you may not often look at very closely."

"I don't review Justin's investment statements. It's enough to keep up with my own."

"Whatever. It's conceivable that they thought they could blackmail Justin over what they could leak to Federal authorities, maybe the press, about his past. Or to you. Probably not that he would go to jail, but that he would be investigated, or his reputation ruined. Perhaps they threatened him and the family with violence. The incident on the parkway could have been a warning."

"It sounds so preposterous, so . . . so . . . It's just crazy, unbelievable. It's something you read in stories, or see in the movies. Made for HBO."

"I know. Many relationships and behaviors go on between people that we never imagine, and never hear about. Then when we do, we say 'how awful. That would never be us.'"

Jackie sat back exhausted. "I don't know what to say. What to think." She looked out the window. It had become dark; traffic had all but disappeared. Snow threatened, although it probably was too cold.

"It's later than I thought we'd be. I need to get home to the children." Jackie got up. "I'll call my house and ask Margaret to stay until I get there and have her start the kids' supper."

"Of course. We lost track of time. I apologize."

"It couldn't be helped. This has been overwhelming."

"I was afraid it would be." Alexis genuinely was concerned. She still wasn't sure how Jackie would resolve all the conflicts raised by what she had heard and discussed that afternoon. She would like to help, but couldn't play both roles.

After Jackie made her call, she sat down once more and looked at Alexis." I need time to think about all this. I just don't know what to tell you. I'm sure I'll have more questions. Can I call you tomorrow?"

"Absolutely. I didn't expect you to come up with an instant response. I'll be here tomorrow. Monday, I'll work at *Stars and Stripes* at the home office down the street. I'm trying to get any kind of lead on Peter for the time in Berlin. Leave a message to call if I'm not here, or we can meet for dinner if you want."

"Maybe you can come to the house. When do you expect to go home? I may not be ready for anything tomorrow."

"I'd hoped for Monday after the newspaper. I've been away more than a week, but you can call me at home. If need be, I can come back up for the day. Don't rush, I'll be close by."

After Jackie left, Alexis sat thinking of the long afternoon. It had gone pretty much as she had envisioned. She believed she'd been fair in what she laid out, and what she withheld. Some of the lingering questions had been answered. Jackie had heard more than enough for now to decide what she wanted next.

Alexis fixed herself a drink from the mini bar and turned on the news. She needed a diversion and to relax before she considered anything about dinner. She wanted to call Luke and Becky before bedtime. She may talk with Travis, although that could wait. Alexis thought fleetingly of her night out in Berlin, a bright spot against the somber story unfolding.

After spending the morning out and about, Alexis had returned to her room. She was putting on her coat ready to leave for an afternoon at the National Gallery when the phone rang. Thinking it might be Jackie, Alexis rushed back to answer. It was Travis. They talked a few minutes and she concluded, "I'll see if I can get a flight down later this afternoon. I think it'll be better that we're both there where he can watch us, and we watch him until we hear from Pat. He flies today. I'll call you before I leave to tell you when to pick me up."

"Sounds good. Sorry to spoil your day."

"Not a problem. I'll let Jackie know, and ask her to call me at home when she decides what she wants. The museum and newspaper can wait. We don't really need to know any more about Peter or Justin."

Alexis checked with the airlines, left a message for Jackie, and checked out of the hotel. A seat was available on the shuttle to Norfolk at five. Thoughtful about the news that had come from Travis, but not alarmed, she looked forward to seeing her children. At the same time, she believed they were entering the end game of their assignment. The trick was going to be to find Justin without compromising him to the very people he had disappeared to lose.

Chapter Twelve

Wednesday afternoon, Alexis drove across the bridge to Currituck. It had been good to get home, and the kids were excited to see her, as were Rags, the small rescue pup, and running pal Leonidas.

The Captain told her he'd come anytime, almost, and not to hesitate to call. The kids were always welcome in St. Augustine. After good by hugs for everyone, he departed for Florida and his boat. Now, she and Travis were meeting to practice on the indoor firing range at the gun club.

Lucas had encouraged Alexis to become comfortable and proficient with her weapon. She rarely carried it then, and had neither taken it out of the locked draw nor practiced for two years since Lucas' death. Upon her return from D.C, Travis insisted she needed to renew her proficiency.

"I know you're a black belt, but there are going to be times when you might need your hand gun," Travis argued.

"I know, I know, that's what Lucas said. I just haven't thought about it, but you're right. Especially now."

Travis wondered if Alexis would actually bring herself to fire at someone even if threatened, but he kept the thought to himself. Nevertheless, he was concerned at the presence of their yet unseen watcher, and the possibility that the man was armed. *More than likely he is. Also, Justin. How will he act towards someone unexpected?* Now watching Alexis, Travis was reassured.

"You're better than I thought you'd be," he remarked as he observed her early rounds. She was rusty, but her form was excellent, and she was self-assured in handling her weapon. "Lucas did a good job with you."

"I knew you'd think I would be skittish.

"He did do a good job. So good that on occasion when we'd compare our targets, I beat him." Alexis knew Travis was doubtful about her martial skills, and she wanted him to feel more comfortable. She appreciated his concern, and was grateful that he had urged her back to the practice range.

He's right, I've been neglectful. However, he does tend to be a bit too macho sometimes. "Are you going to shoot? Once I get back to where I was, we'll compete; you may need to practice."

"Yeah, yeah," he laughed. "Just let me know when you're ready."

Travis left to work the bar at Safe Port while Alexis went home to fix dinner. Driving up the road to the house, she noticed a car parked in the drive at the Murchison's on the left, a couple of houses down. She wondered if it was the watcher since the house was closed for the winter. Worried, she parked outside the garage and was greeted by Leonidas.

The phone was ringing as she came in the door.

"Alexis here."

"Hi, Alexis. It's Jackie." Her tone was both subdued and defiant. "I would have called sooner, but I just couldn't stop thinking. Then I went to see Louis yesterday, and was completely stonewalled. He flatly denies that he knows anything about Justin's disappearance, or why. He's very kind, very competent, and very convincing, but whether it's the truth or not, it doesn't help me." She waited for Alexis to reply.

"I know how difficult it is. It was difficult to reveal to you what we uncovered. Do you want me to come up and talk?"

"Not now. I called to tell you to continue trying to find Justin. If he's alive, I want to find out why he abandoned me and the children, and what he has in mind about the future of our marriage. The deceptions certainly have changed everything."

Alexis nodded. She wasn't surprised. She wished she could tell Jackie they knew Justin was alive and were getting close, but she knew it was premature. Now that Jackie had confronted Louis, and with the presence of their watcher there on the Banks, the situation was even more delicate. "How much did you reveal to Louis about what I told you? Does he know I'm working for you?"

"Nothing specific. I described to him the events I told you. I said I'd been thinking about them, that I thought they were connected, and that maybe Justin hadn't told me everything about the investigation. Louis downplayed it all, and said my imagination was running away with me. He told me he knew it was difficult, but he was sure there was another more plausible explanation. He said I had to be patient.

"Alexis, he just made me angry. Especially since you've pretty well confirmed that everything is connected. My imagination is running away with me! Thanks a lot. And a more plausible explanation. Such as what?"

While Jackie had moved more to the defiant end of the scale, Alexis was back to wondering just how much Louis knew of Justin's dilemma and what story Justin had concocted to get the lawyer's support. At least he didn't yet know about her, and that was a relief.

"Jackie, your anger is understandable, but don't blame Louis too much. Remember, we don't know if he's covering for Justin, or what he knows about the situation.

"Now that you indicate you want me to go on, Travis and I will move more aggressively to uncover and explore some leads to discover what's happened. Travis picked up some information during his last visit to your home, and we are checking it out. Meanwhile, do your best to maintain. Try to find some outlet for all your stress and frustration. Do you have a health club or something? It would be better than punching out Louis."

Jackie laughed. "I can always count on you to bring me back from the brink. I'll try to follow your advice.

"Actually, Justin and I played tennis with some other couples at an indoor court nearby. Maybe I can get together with one or two of the wives.

"You're right; it would be good for me. I've avoided friends because I didn't know what to say about Jus, and I was worried about how they'd treat me. I'll think about how to handle it, or maybe get someone at work go to the health club downtown close to the gallery."

"Both sound like good ideas. I'll keep in touch with any progress, and you call me anytime." Alexis hated to think what Jackie would say if she knew how much had been held back. *Oh well, that's how it goes in the business. Louis and I actually have something in common.* In the end, some details would not be revealed.

Outside, it was a dreary February afternoon and almost dark. Alexis wasn't enthusiastic about the postponed run, but she felt the need to unwind. Also she was recharged to know they could move forward with the case, and got ready to go out with Leonidas who was eagerly pacing at the door. Later she would discuss the situation with Travis and see if they could make contact with Pat.

"Yeah, he's back, but I tell you there's nothing here that says he's connected to the Feds or anyone. The past couple of nights he filled in at a bar. His story that he was helping find that lady's husband up in D.C. is a possibility, but he does very little here. He's retired Navy. Works the dive scene in the summers like I told you." JP, the Miami guy, was talking again to Toronto. This time he was using the phone from inside the hotel just off the lobby. He didn't know why Toronto didn't want him to call from his motel; it had to be a pay phone. *These guys are a bit wacko.*

"He doesn't look like he's getting ready to go anywhere. He's been in the woman's office in Kitty Hawk a couple times for a few hours; otherwise he stays pretty much in his apartment over the garage. He's probably waiting out winter."

"Kitty Hawk. What a place to have an office." Hoping to be released from the desolate place he asked, "You think it's worth hanging around any longer? The guy's no big deal." JP was thinking of mild Miami with its hot night life.

"What? What? Why?" JP was stunned. He listened to the other end. "Is it really necessary? This isn't a very good place to pull off something like that." He listened some more, thinking of the limited options for getting out of the area, let alone finding a convenient place for what they wanted. Travis may be laid back, but he wasn't a fool, from what Miami and Toronto had told him.

"Are you sure?" he argued one more time knowing it was futile. JP was convinced these guys were wacko. However, his Miami bosses told him to follow orders from Toronto. *But it's my neck at stake. Shit.*

"I'll let you know." He hung up. He didn't like it. He wondered if it would do any good to call Miami, but dismissed that as futile. He decided to call and let them know what was up. This was going to be tricky.

* * *

"Alexis, Travis here." He recorded on her answering machine. "I'm on the way to the office to pick up Mac, and we're off to Avon to finish the job. We'll spend the night in Buxton. I made a big show of picking up my gear from the dive shop and taking it to the apartment as we planned. Will be on the job in Hatteras tomorrow morning. Let you know if anything is up."

After stopping for gas and stocking up on beer and snacks, Travis met up with Mac, another technician, at the security office in Kitty Hawk. Using the beach road, they drove in the direction of Highway 12. A green Honda pulled into traffic a short distance behind. Once past the ranger station at the gateway to the Cape Hatteras National Seashore, there was little traffic and winter bleakness stretched on either side.

"You see that Honda behind us? Is it the one we picked up after leaving the office?" Travis was riding shotgun and watching in the side view mirror.

"I think so." Mac responded with a shrug. "What did you say might be going on?" They were nearing the Bodie Lighthouse turnoff. Winds were quiet and a pale sun was obscured by slate skies. Nothing stirred in the marshes, brown and stark, as they approached the Oregon Inlet Bridge.

Back in Southern Shores, Alexis finished making flight reservations to St. Kitts. Pat had called and said it was time for Travis to join him. She hoped once he left, the shadowy watcher would leave as well. The man was creepy, and she worried about Becky and Luke.

Since Monday night at the bar, Travis sighted the man three times, watching him from a distance. At least twice, the green Honda was parked in the Murchison's drive as well. With Travis and Mac on the way south, Alexis hoped that the man would follow them, or at least stay away from the house.

The watcher should be bored out of his mind by now. When Travis leaves for St. Kitts with his equipment, it'll appear that he's off somewhere diving. At least that was the plan. From the crosswalk to the office, Alexis looked down the street at the summer neighbor's house. *I want the creep out of here.*

The next morning, in pre-dawn Alexis was out of the house. A cold wind blew from the northeast, and she pulled her jacket around her as she got into the Land Rover. She left a note for the children, and set out their breakfast. She would call from the car later to be sure they were up and ready for school.

Alexis was concerned by Travis' request as she thought about the call last night from Buxton. He and Mac had been followed by their watcher. They saw him in a diner, so he must be staying over.

"Alexis, I think I'm being stalked, not just watched. Mac and I entered the diner, and I happened to catch his eyes. He's a killer."

"That sounds bad, Travis. Is there something I can do?" It wasn't the kind of evidence she normally expected from him, but trusting his instincts she didn't question further.

"We're set to do the job at Hatteras around eight. Can you bring my hand gun up to the motel early tomorrow morning? Just in case."

Alexis had slept badly. She couldn't believe Travis was being stalked for a killing. It didn't make sense, but she brought her pistol along as well.

Dawn was just appearing when she pulled into the OB Motel in Buxton. The damp fog covered everything with a salt air film. She found the firm's service truck parked under the building. The door was unlocked as Travis told her it would be; she slipped his gun under the seat. Then she drove toward Hatteras looking for an open cafe where she could get some breakfast.

Thirty minutes later, fortified with breakfast, Alexis drove to the end of the island. The job was at a newly finished house across from the ferry dock where Highway 12 continued by water to Okracoke. Alexis found she could keep an eye on it from an edge of the shopping center parking lot next to the motel. She positioned her car and called home. According to Luke, both he and Becky were up and almost ready for school.

"What are you doing in Hatteras, Mom?"

"I had to come down early to help Travis and Mac on a project. I'll be back by the time you get home. Don't miss the bus."

"Why did they need you this early?"

"Travis asked me to bring something they forgot. I left lunch money for both of you on the table. Don't forget to let Rags out to pee and bring him in. Have to hang up."

To kill time, Alexis went into a store with a takeout deli and ordered more coffee. She hated waiting, it was boring, but Travis wanted her to keep her eye on him and Mac. Alexis appreciated his attempt to downplay his sense of concern, but she wasn't fooled. Travis was worried. *Well Stalker, I'm on the lookout for you.* She sipped her coffee and read a morning paper.

It was windy at the dock. They were at the end of the Cape where winds often were the worse. A ferry was unloading commuters from Okracoke along with some small service vehicles. A small line of cars waited to load.

On the way out to the Rover, Alexis saw who she thought was the blond watcher approaching the deli cafe from across the lot. She ducked her head, turning left along the walkway of shops. She pulled her cap closer to her face, hoping he didn't notice her. Travis and Mac had arrived at the house across the street, their van parked in the drive. Alexis called Travis on her cell phone from the car.

"I think our friend followed you to the site. He's in getting coffee or breakfast. I'm across the street at the edge of the lot."

"It's good to hear your voice. Thanks for the delivery."

"I'll stay here as long as you want. What have you told Mac?"

"I told him some creep is watching me, and there may be trouble. He's worried about it, but cool. If something looks bad, he'll get out of the way."

"I hope you're wrong about this. The guy knows there're two of you, and I don't want Mac to find himself in the middle. What would I say to his wife and little girl if something happened?"

"Neither do I. I hope I'm wrong also. Let me know when he comes out."

Alexis nervously checked the number for the sheriff's office in her contact list, and scrunched into a position so she could keep her eye on the store while appearing to read her paper. Binoculars and a pistol rested within reach on the seat next to her. Twenty minutes slipped by.

Preparations were underway to load the ferry to go the other way when the man came out and went to his car. Alexis watched him closely. He had his head tucked down against the wind and appeared oblivious to her Rover. He drove out onto the road and around the shrub divide to pass the building where Travis and Mac were working. A few minutes later, he came back and passed again slowly. He drove toward the end of the Cape.

Alexis called Travis. "He's casing out the building. He's been by twice."

"Where is he now?"

"Off towards the end of the road. Is there an approach from the back?"

"Not by car. I looked around this morning after we got here. If he wants to come that way, he'll have to walk across cactus-infested sand."

"Where are you in the building?"

"We started downstairs. Maybe we'll move up. I'll tell Mac to get in the bathroom and lock himself in if anything starts."

"That's a good idea. I'll call when anything changes." Alexis rubbed her arms and stamped her feet. It was freezing in the car. She decided to turn on the engine and get some heat. *Maybe I should alert the sheriff.*

Minutes later the Honda returned. It passed the drive, stopped, and began backing in. Alexis reached for her phone.

"Travis, he's parking in the drive. I'm calling the police. He'll be out of the car soon. Are you ready?"

"We're upstairs. Thanks for the warning."

Alexis dialed the number for the sheriff's office. Her hands were shaking.

"Sheriff's office."

"This is Alexis Mason. There's a scene involving guns developing here at the new house across from the ferry. We need police." *Should I have called sooner?*

"I'll send someone out there right away. Where are you?"

"In the parking lot of the shopping center next to the line up for the ferry."

"Listen! A white service truck and a dark green Honda are parked in the driveway to the house. Two men are inside working. One is armed. Another who's entering the building is armed as well."

"We're calling dispatch right now."

Alexis hung up. She already was moving out of the lot. She hoped the officers would be quick. The Hatteras Division of the sheriff's office was just two miles down the road in the small town, but the patrol car could be anywhere.

Putting all other thoughts aside, she checked her weapon, got out, and slipped to the front of the car. From that vantage she could see the front door to the building was ajar. Alexis stretched forward peering in vain for sign of the gunman. She approached cautiously. Just inside, she listened. It was eerily quiet. She thought she heard a sound on the stairs. She waited.

"Freeze," the voice came from upstairs. Alexis was moving to the stairs when a shot sounded. An object clattered to the floor as a second shot fired buckling the leg of the man with one foot on the last stair and one on the landing. He fell sprawling forward. Alexis saw Travis kick away a gun. She looked at her own still warm in her hand, and thought of Lucas, who had insisted that she learn to shoot.

Chapter Thirteen

Shortly after his arrival on the island, Pat situated himself in Basseterre across the street and down two buildings from the bank identified by Justin's call to his lawyer. He had a scope focused on the front entrance from his window, but the main surveillance, in fact, was in the hands of a vendor who set up his cart each day on the street directly in front.

So far, none of his inquiries had turned up the slightest hint that a man fitting Justin's description had taken up residence on St. Kitts. Thinking that Justin might be staying in Nevis, a nearby island, Pat called for Travis so they could expand the search.

"I'm glad you got here. Was there any problem leaving so quickly after the shooting?" Pat greeted Travis at the airport and helped carry his gear to the car.

"Not really. I spent a couple of hours answering questions, gave the police my statement, and left yesterday morning. Talked to the FBI who came right away when I said drugs were involved. They didn't say anything about sticking around, and I didn't ask. If there's any problem, Alexis can handle it." Travis had arrived just before noon after spending the night in Miami.

Pat parked near the marina and the two went in for lunch at a small cafe overlooking the water. They sipped beer while waiting for their sandwiches. "I've worked the island," Pat said, "but with all the tourists it's been hard. I'll keep looking here and watch the bank, but there's a chance he could be holed up in Nevis." Pat pointed vaguely over the water. From what I've been told, it may be easier for someone to find a place there to lay low. It's only a short trip by boat."

"So I'll go over there and check it out. No problem. If I do find him, you'll have to come over too." Travis was eager to get started on the hunt, but was not prepared for what Pat was telling him. When leaving North Carolina, he thought Pat had all but located Justin.

"First, you need to rent a car. That way you can haul your gear with you. It'll be easier than waiting until you're there."

"Can I get it done today?"

"Probably. Let's get started." Pat was frustrated by his limited headway in the search.

Later in the day, Travis cased out the dock area and checked the ferry schedule. He was ready to make his trip to Nevis the next morning, two miles south across the water. Squinting in the sun, he could just make out the cone-capped island. It was smaller and quieter than St. Kitts, and Travis hoped the search would not be as complicated and inconclusive as it had been until now. Justin must be on one of these two islands. He could be dangerously exposed by traveling to the bank from somewhere else. Pat and he agreed on this.

Landing off the ferry at Charlestown the next morning, Travis cruised the streets in his rented Jeep. He covered the small town quickly, admiring along the way the wide quiet streets lined with long standing houses built with locally quarried volcanic stone, and shaded by West Indian fretted verandas. At first glance, he reflected, it was difficult to tell that Nevis, once a prosperous sugar plantation colony and birthplace of Alexander Hamilton, was now the registered location for thousands of offshore businesses operating under strict secrecy laws.

Too early to look for a room, Travis began a leisurely tour of the small island, deciding to case out the terrain as he initiated the search for Justin. Along the way, he planned to stop in some villages, and ask about the man in the photo he carried. He was traveling as a tourist with scuba gear in the back of the car. *Maybe not be the best cover for the job, but what the heck, get on with it.*

The twenty some mile trip around the island lasted about four hours, counting all the stops, including such villages as Gingerland and New River. No one he spoke with recognized the man in the photo, whom Travis described as a diving buddy some friends had told him recently came to the area. However, he did pick up suggestions from the locals about where people looking for a low-key, long term residence might inquire. By the time he was back in Charlestown, he knew what his next steps would entail. He found a room in a quiet hotel not far from the ferry dock and moved his gear inside.

Three days later in early light, Travis stood on a dock at Oualie Beach watching Pat pull into a slip. He hopped on the deck, took a line, and jumped back to fasten it to a post. With a wave, Pat cut the engine.

Travis joined Pat in the cabin. "Good to see you. Any trouble getting the boat?"

"None at all. I already had one lined up before you arrived just in case we might need it."

Travis stowed his gear and made a quick check on the tank Pat had brought. The men walked to a nearby cafe for breakfast, and to discuss the day's agenda.

Once they ordered, Travis began his report with cryptic description. "The house is over on the east coast, Atlantic side. The water's rough over there, and the beaches are shallow and rocky. Not many people other than residents in the private houses tucked away. I've got a chart and marked what may be Justin's location.

When we get there, we'll case out what the conditions are for an approach, and then decide the best way for me to go in. I'll probably go without the tank and take my stuff in a pouch. I don't know if there are steps to the beach, so I may have to climb." Travis unfolded a navigation chart of the waters around the island and pointed to the area off shore from what he thought was Justin's sanctuary.

"You did a good job of uncovering him." Pat was impressed. "I thought it might take longer."

"I had less area to cover and fewer tourists to confuse the scene than you. The person who handled the lease is certain the man in the picture is the same one he dealt with, although Justin is now sporting a short well groomed beard. If I'm able, I'll get a picture with my camera to confirm that it's Justin. I'm hoping that getting up to the house from the beach won't be too tricky, and there'll be some cover once I'm at the top."

"You said you cased it out from land. Could you tell much?" Pat put the chart aside to dig into his breakfast.

"Not much. The grounds are enclosed on three sides by walls about six feet with jagged rocks on top. There's a gate which is probably armed to a system inside the house. The house is well back and obscured by palms. I couldn't make out much. He has a groundskeeper and housekeeper who live in a small cabin on the property. The guy may double as a guard of some kind. Locals say that sort of arrangement is pretty common for the people who own and rent these houses. I didn't want to draw attention to myself, so didn't stay very long."

"So if it's our man, he's locked in pretty tight." Pat summed up thoughtfully.

"Not ultra tight, but private and low key. Moderate deterrents against unwanted intruders. He's probably not expecting anyone to track him, but wants to stay reclusive and anonymous. It's a pretty good set up. He's been clever in changing his identity, and tucking away. Calls himself Carter Richards."

Travis and Pat continued to discuss the situation and game plan as they ate. "Have you been in touch with Alexis yet?"

"I'm waiting until after today. I'd like to be sure before I call for her to come." Always the charmer, Travis smiled at the waitress who refilled his cup. "Did you put any food on board? We're going to want some grub before the day is over. The swim alone will work up an appetite."

"I didn't have a chance. I only had time to bring the tank. I thought we'd do it here."

"That's fine. We'd better get going then." They cleared their plates with one last swipe of toast, swallowed a couple more gulps of coffee, and got up to pay the check. As they left the restaurant, the sun rose over the quiet Caribbean isle.

* * *

Alexis flew from Dare County Airport into General Aviation at Dulles. It was a clear cloudless day. The trip had been hastily arranged after she talked with Travis the night before. He said it was time for her to come to St. Kitts. This was the signal that Justin had been located. Before confronting Justin, she and Jackie were meeting one more time at a quiet restaurant in Georgetown. Alexis knew it would be a difficult encounter.

Sitting in a private alcove, the two women ordered and had the waiter bring each a glass of wine. Jackie was cordial, but obviously tense. After exchanging small talk, Jackie spoke first. "I've had a long talk with Philip, and he confirmed the facts about Justin's dealings in Berlin. It was uncomfortable and strained; he's had a hard time accepting me."

Jackie sat back in her chair and continued. "However, he insists that the part about the drugs is only speculation. His mother and Matthias admit that, although they consider it credible."

"That's correct." Alexis was surprised at the opening. "But more has happened since we last met to confirm that Peter, at least, is connected to drug dealers now, and they are behind whatever prompted the meetings with Justin." This was not the direction she expected to take. Obviously, Jackie had been doing some serious thinking.

"Either way," Jackie replied firmly, "it's clear that Justin's not the person I thought he was. You said you've confirmed he's alive? Where is he?"

Alexis sorted through the last statement. This would be trickier than she anticipated. "We don't know yet," she lied. "We're still looking. We know he's alive because we've been able to trace his money which was moved from a numbered account he has in Luxembourg." Alexis decided to stretch the truth.

"I needed to meet with you to explain we know he's being sought by the drug group working out of Toronto. To reveal his location could put him in danger; to reveal it to you could put you and the children in danger as well. When we find him we'll protect his location. We'll approach him carefully. I came to hear what message you want me to convey to him."

"I asked you to find him. Do you intend not to tell me where he is?"

"When it appears safe for you to know. I need to talk with Justin first. What do you want to say to him?" The conversation was becoming more difficult.

Jackie stared at Alexis. Without answering the question she stated, "I'm very concerned about the danger. I've started to think about taking the children out of here for awhile, Maybe Florence, if some sort of exchange can be arranged through the gallery. Aren't you worried about your children? I would never have gotten you involved if I believed it would expose you to so much violence."

For the first time Alexis could smile reassuringly. "The sheriff and local police are keeping a careful lookout down where I am, and I wouldn't be surprised if the FBI had someone on the ground there as well. For now, I'm not worried." The two women finished their lunch in silence, each sifting through their thoughts. They ordered desert, trading small questions and comments.

"I appreciate everything you've done to find Justin, although the truth has turned out to be . . . difficult," Jackie said, searching for the right word while refilling their cups. She paused, looking away in thought, and then looked again at Alexis. "When you find Justin, tell him I pray for his safety." Jackie took a deep breath. "But tell him," she paused again, "everything has changed between us and I doubt that we have a future together." Trying to control her voice she continued, "I understand that he may think he's made mistakes, yet can justify them. But it doesn't change the fact that he's been deceptive and dishonest with me. He's clearly not the Justin I thought he was."

Alexis said nothing.

Daylight hours were getting longer once more, and as Alexis flew south she thought she may get home before dark. Flying over Virginia, few signs remained of the snow and ice from the storm three weeks before, except on the Blue Ridge Mountains in the distance. She was deeply bothered by her meeting with Jackie. She understood Jackie's feelings and was saddened by her decision. At the same time, Alexis felt sympathy for Justin, who believed he had put the past behind him, and by a fluke of fortune it caught up with him.

* * *

Alexis followed a narrow, hard-packed road out of town in the rented Jeep, watching carefully for the landmarks provided by Travis. As she reached the other side of the island, she caught occasional glimpses of the ocean through the palms and low lying undergrowth. She reached the stone wall and recessed gate. Stepping out of the car, ignoring the sign 'Please Ring', she pulled up the latch and swung it open. Somewhere inside the house an alarm rang. Alexis boldly drove up the drive.

Walking around the house to the ocean side, Alexis approached the veranda where she might find Justin who, according to Travis, took lunch there at this time. She didn't expect Justin would be pleased, but she didn't anticipate violence. Beyond that, she wasn't sure of anything. By now, Travis, approaching by way of the beach, should be in place.

Alexis wondered which Justin she was about to confront: Justin the engaging and successful man she thought she knew, or Justin the black marketer, drug courier, and possible killer? She hoped to stay outside where Travis could keep his eye on them and take pictures of the meeting to show Jackie. Travis also would cover her with the scoped rifle he asked her to bring when she flew into Nevis. Alexis thought about the groundskeeper and his wife and the alarm she set off coming in the gate.

Justin was reading a newspaper when she stepped up on the patio veranda, his lunch barely touched. He looked up at her approach and sat up startled, pushing away from the table. Alexis, careful to keep her hands open and in front, smiled as she walked towards him, just as she would when greeting him at home.

"Hello, Justin. You have a beautiful place here. The view is spectacular. It's wonderful to find you alive."

Justin remained in place. He sat back in his chair, and warily watched her finish her approach. "Alexis Mason. Where the fuck did you come from? How did you know I was here?" his questions reflected anger and alarm. He looked around as if expecting one of his servants.

"Jackie asked me to help find out what happened to you. She's had a terrible time dealing with your disappearance: whether you're alive or dead." Alexis wanted her presence explained quickly to reduce Justin's alarm. She continued, "The police haven't found a trace of you or your car. Your attorney convinced her not to get private investigators involved or to pursue a missing person report. But she refused to just sit back and do nothing. So she turned to me. She trusts me, and knew I'd keep it low key."

Justin simply stared at her, trying to absorb it all. Alexis smiled in a way she hoped was reassuring, and stood quietly, giving him time to react. The groundskeeper stepped out from an arch shielding a door from the kitchen holding a small hand gun in one hand. Alexis thought of Travis whom she hoped was nearby.

"Mr. Richards, this stranger drove through the gate without ringing. I came as quickly as I could."

Justin looked at his groundskeeper and back at Alexis who stood relaxed showing no alarm. "Its okay, Miguel, the lady's an acquaintance. You got here in good time. Please ask Christina to bring Mrs. Mason a glass of ice tea and . . ." he turned to Alexis, "Would you like a salad, a sandwich?"

"No thank you," she said looking back at Justin, "Tea would be nice." Alexis moved to the table. She was intensely focused, but felt a sense of surreal. Tea? A sandwich? Justin, the perfect host.

"Just tea then and see that the gate is secure. Keep your eye on the drive until Mrs. Mason leaves," Justin nodded to Miguel. He turned back to his unexpected guest.

"Sit down, Alexis. This is a surprise, a serious matter, you being here." The sun glittered off an aqua blue ocean, while a warm breeze softly ruffled the palms shading the veranda and yard.

"Tell me about your remarkable feat of finding me." Justin spoke casually, but Alexis detected a hard edge in his voice he could not disguise.

"It's not necessary to go into all the details. Jackie called me in December just before Christmas. She was close to a breakdown. I went up and listened to what she had to say, starting with your sudden trip to New York. Then about the phone calls late at night and the accident on the parkway. Finally, she told of the hunting trip that didn't take place, but ended with your disappearance. She asked me, actually hired me, to try to find out what happened to you." Alexis paused and waited for a reaction from Jus who was biting into his lunch, his expression inscrutable behind dark glasses. He drank some tea, pursed his lips, and looked at her.

"And what brought you to here," he finally asked.

Alexis smiled. "Hard work," she answered with a hint of relaxed confidence.

"Hard work," he repeated. "And have you reported it to Jackie?"

"Not yet." She was going to give him only a little at a time as they maneuvered to the main issue.

"Not yet. Why the delay?"

Christina brought Alexis a glass of ice tea, placed a plate of fresh fruit on the table, and then quickly returned to the kitchen.

Alexis waited until she left and responded, "She knows I'm close, but I told her I had to talk with you once you were located."

"And why is that?" Justin shifted in his chair knocking his plate on the glass table. A gecko scurried across the edge of the veranda startling them both.

Alexis picked up again. "You must realize that in the course of the hard work, the probability of you being in danger from others looking for you has been well noted. I've reported to your wife that alive or dead your motive for not including her in your confidence might be a matter of trying to shield her from pressure or threat from the same people."

Justin put down the sandwich. He no longer tried to appear casual; a slight frown crossed his brow. "Does anyone else know you're looking for me? "Unfortunately, yes," she was going to be frank. "In trying to track down Peter, my colleague encountered hostile behavior from some people in Toronto. They followed him to Carolina and tried to kill him. Now, I believe the FBI is looking into the drug situation in Toronto with the Canadian authorities. Travis had to tell them about Peter's connection up there which led to all the violence. I also talked with Anna and Matthias in Berlin." She summarized quickly. At the mention of Peter, Justin's demeanor hardened. Through the glasses, she could barely see his menacing stare.

"Toronto, Berlin. You have been working hard. Anywhere else?"

Alexis dropped another name, "Not to Dresden, if that's what you mean." She almost could feel his recoil. Yet Jus held his composure.

Not acknowledging the mention of Dresden, Justin asked, "What about Philip?"

Alexis almost felt sorry for him as he realized he was revealed to those whom meant the most. "I spoke to Philip once, so he knows Jackie called me in. He was there when Jackie took me to your office. However, he was in touch with Matthias before I got to Berlin. Your sons are very concerned. I don't think Jackie has said much to Philip herself, except to confirm some of the facts I learned from Anna." she let Justin know the worst.

Justin continued to frown. He eyed her through his sunglasses. She couldn't read him well through the dark lenses, but could feel his hostility. Maybe a rising mood of fear.

"You are as clever as Lucas said you were. He always said I underestimated you."

"You think all women are ornaments," she shot back.

Justin sipped his drink and sat back. "No. No, I don't. Not really," he said thoughtfully as if the matter had never been put to him. "Anna was very competent and Jackie is as well, although their temperament and interests are different." He paused again thinking. "It's just that I always viewed you as Lucas' Mrs. Lieutenant and couldn't make the shift when the two of you started working together." He reached again for his glass. His sandwich remained unfinished on the plate. A pause. "I guess I do have a blind spot about women," he conceded. Another hesitation. "And here we are, Mrs. PI."

"Do you know that Peter also has disappeared?"

Justin set his mouth firmly and frowned again. He spoke guardedly, "If that is true, I'm not surprised Peter has disappeared. The little shit let them use him to extort money from me and then double-crossed them. That's why I took the measures I did and why I'm here now. They should focus on finding him."

Alexis was taken back by the fierceness of his statement. The accusation about Peter didn't fit the sequence she and Travis had pieced together leading to Justin's disappearance. Unless he expected to pay once and disappear to deny them a chance to push him for more. But why did Justin think or know that Peter had double crossed his runners?

After a pause to process what was just suggested Alexis said softly, "You hope his associates will think he got rid of you, and took the money for himself. Without him, who will they have to pressure you in the future?"

Justin half smiled. "Something like that." He stood up and walked over to the railing facing the sea.

"It was crazy. You can't imagine. Crazy! Concocting a threat over something that occurred years ago to extort money from me. Me! Justin Lawrence. My money! Money I earned with careful investment and grew with good enterprise management. Uncle Martin said my father finally would be pleased with me." Justin stood looking out, his back to Alexis waiting quietly. Gathering his composure, he turned and returned to the table.

"I guess Jackie told you about meeting Karl in Dresden." Justin sat back trying to look relaxed. "Whoever Karl rustled out of the bushes in Dresden could not possibly be the ones he dealt with in the eighties. It wasn't like he had direct connections then to Marcus Wolf. Probable a low level Stasi operative at best. Maybe there was some possible link, but, God! What a damn crock." His bitterness seared the air between them.

Without waiting for a response Justin continued, "The important thing at this time is that Jackie and Philip, not anyone, can know where I am in case they're being watched. You must see that. Eventually, with Peter missing, they'll give it up."

Alexis sat stunned. A sudden breeze rustled the leaves of the bushes and palms in a fluttering sweep. She looked out toward the ocean wondering how close Travis was to the veranda. Could he hear any of this conversation?

"Those types might still kill you just for the insult. Do you realize how frightened and lost Jackie is? She's holding it together for the children and her self-respect. She knows you haven't been honest with her. She feels betrayed, and told me to tell you that she has doubts about the future with you." Alexis paused unsure, and then decided to push harder. "And she doesn't realize you took a gun with you from your collection." The violent scenes in Berlin and Virginia coupled with the missing gun flashed like snap shots through Alexis' thoughts. It seemed incredible that the amiable man sitting there, holding his iced tea glass in well manicured hands, was a killer. She shivered slightly in the warm sun.

Justin's face hardened again. He looked at her with cold malice and leaned towards her, "Just what are you suggesting?" Alexis continued to sit relaxed. She reached for her tea hoping to show calm while holding his glare.

"You have a lot of repair work on the home front to do if you hope to save your relationship. That's without anything that might come up over Peter's disappearance." She took a long sip and set down the glass. Though outwardly calm, her mouth was dry, and the cool liquid tasted good.

Justin reached across and grabbed her wrist firmly. "Are the police looking for Peter's whereabouts, or even think that there's been a crime?"

Alexis didn't flinch and held her ground. "They are sniffing around in Toronto. And they know that Peter was involved in contacts with you." She wondered if she was pressing the point too hard.

"Of course, he's a small fry as far as things going on in Toronto. The authorities wouldn't have much interest in him." Alexis tried to sound reassuring and helpful.

"You were hired to find me. You succeeded. Congratulations. You've done an extraordinary job. But that means others can as well. I may have to relocate. You realize that?" He relaxed the grip slightly on her wrist, and leaned closer across the table starring at her through his glasses. Alexis could tell his eyes were squinted. She could smell his cologne. She wondered if he considered her a liability like Peter.

"How did you let yourself get so involved in those activities in Berlin? Did you ever think of the consequences?" Alexis couldn't help herself. Justin's audacity was more than she expected.

Justin leaned back and smiled, his anger subsiding. "Not much." he admitted. "I took some chances that were foolish which I regret, but overall not much. Hell, it was the get-rich Eighties. Everyone was on the make. I didn't want to be a left-behind schmuck. I used the money to fund investments. Besides," he leaned forward again, "it was fifteen years ago. It's over. Past. No one cares about it now." Justin stopped and composed himself once again.

"Look. Report to your client that I'm alive and in hiding until I think it's safe. She's not to tell anyone, not even Phillip. Especially not our children. I did what I had to do so they would be safe. There was no other way. It's wrong for them to be caught up in something that was over long ago. Jackie must understand. The situation may take awhile for things to ease back to normal." Justin's tone carried a message of anger, conflict, and resignation.

Alexis stared back for a moment, with the breeze softly brushing her face; the faint sound of the ocean roughing the beach reaching them in the silence. She was shocked at Justin's callous justification for his actions. She realized that Jackie's message hadn't sunk in, if he had even heard it. She felt it was time to leave.

Alexis withdrew her arm from Justin's grip and stood up. "Thank you for the tea. I'll convey your message. Your view of the ocean is lovely. You must see mine someday." She thought the statements absurd, but a way to retreat. She walked to the stairs almost fearful to turn her back. When she reached the bottom step, she looked back to see Justin at the top watching.

* * *

Flying across the Caribbean towards Florida, the sea shimmered through occasional clouds. Small specks of pleasure boats and cruise liners moved far below. Travis was asleep in one of the passenger seats, his gear thrown in a heap on another. Alexis wished he'd be more careful with her plane. She sighed and thought of her encounter with Justin.

Jus was right. Whatever had become of Peter, Justin wasn't under suspicion for any crime. He has "disappeared," but disappearing is not a crime. The money transfers were with his money. All his affairs are in order. Jackie and the children are provided with everything they need. Philip and Justin's managers are running the business. Louis is taking care of the rest.

Looking down at the sea, now softer in the increasing twilight, endless and peaceful, Alexis began to consider the difficult task ahead. *What am I going to say to Jackie? Huh? Well first, tell her of Justin's location and caution her again of the danger he faces.* Finding Justin was the job she had accepted.

Next on the list, deliver Justin's message to Jackie. Alexis shivered thinking of Justin's callous dismissal of Peter and the justification for his criminal actions. Once again, she visualized the menacing glare behind the dark glasses and shook her head as though to clear it of all the thoughts. Still they continued.

Later when it appears safe, Justin and Jackie might make contact. What if Jackie asks her to act as liaison? Will she accept that role? Alexis sighed. *I don't think so.*

Will we ever know what happened to Peter? The final question.

"*Scheisse.*" Alexis said aloud. "There could be a lot more bones in that schrank of Justin's than any of us imagine." Travis stirred in the seat behind at the sound of her voice.

The sun continued to sink into darkness across the quiet Caribbean. In Berlin, it was the middle of the night. Streets were empty at the site of a long gone Checkpoint Charlie; lights reflected fuzzy in the wet dark. Not far away, years ago, Conrad Schumann jumped the wire, Peter Fechter bled to death in no-man's land and down the block Justin Lawrence transported drugs from the East for easy money.

It would be many weeks before spring with leaves on the trees at the zoo and along Unter den Linden. Another cold front was on the way. A light icy drizzle mixed with snow fell on Friedrichstrasse.

Epilogue

November 2000: North Carolina

Cooled down and changed from her morning run, Alexis was pouring herself coffee when Rags barked at the sound of a car pulling up in the driveway. Leonidas seconded the challenge from the ocean front porch. Moving quickly to the door, she opened it to greet FBI agent Russ Benson.

"Russ. What a surprise. What brings you down?"

"Good morning Alexis. Sorry to come unannounced. I was sent to speak with you. May I come in?" The previous February, Russ led the investigating team after a drug cartel hit man was captured following a shoot out in Hatteras which had involved Travis and Alexis.

Coffee in hand the two stood outside overlooking the Atlantic as November wind brushed the sand. Sea oats danced on the dunes amidst the live oak cover.

"A decomposed body was discovered by two hunters in the Adirondacks near Chestertown a couple of weeks ago. Their dogs found it partially dug up in a shallow grave."

Alexis suppressed a shudder of alarm. "Wow." She uttered half under her breath. "Why have you come to me? Has it been identified?" Leonidas leaped down the steps to the yard in pursuit of a rabbit he spied scurrying into the live oak underbrush.

* * *

April 2000: Nevis Island

Standing on the veranda looking toward the sea, Justin could hear the low engine murmur from a Zodiac tender approaching the shallow beach. Darkness was closing in and the water, translucent blue close to shore during the day, now appeared opaque and black. The yacht anchored beyond the cove was not visible from where he stood, but he knew it was there waiting for his arrival.

Christina emerged from a nearby entrance to the veranda and signaled that it was time for him to leave. Taking a final look around, Justin descended the stairs and with reluctant step ambled across the lawn. Focused and careful, he navigated the narrow pathway to the beach, realizing that his departure signified what might well be an on-going flight. The recent meeting with Jackie, hastily arranged, had not gone well, and within days he decided his location was too compromised to remain in Nevis.

Miguel already was assisting with the loading of luggage and when Justin reached the tender, he handed his laptop and satchel over to be taken on as well. Small waves slapped against the Zodiac lifting it in an agitated motion. Justin could barely sight the yacht anchored less than a mile out, identified by dim interior lights.

A handshake followed by an embrace for Miguel, Carter Richards, now Barton Charles, jump-stepped onto the side and down into the inflatable transport. A hand was offered from one of the crew to help him aboard. The idling Yamaha motor clunked into reverse pulling the boat into the choppy surf and turned toward open water. Shifting into forward, the engine quickly picked up speed and the Zodiac headed steadily toward the waiting craft. By nightfall the yacht was underway.

* * *

"We're working on that." Russ leaned over the rail to see where Leonidas had disappeared. "At first the two hunters, Ron Creighton and Martin Gavin, thought the body may be that of their friend Justin Lawrence who has been missing for almost a year. Once that proved false neither of them could speculate on who it may be." The agent, brow slightly arched, looked at Alexis.

"Eventually the state police called us in. The two hunters repeated their story to our agents in New York which included your inquiry last winter about Justin's disappearance. When your name was plugged into the system, it popped up in our files connected to the case down here. I was sent over to follow up."

Ron and Martin. What an awful shock. But why would they think it may be Justin? And Jackie. She's living in Florence with the children. Did she ever make contact with Justin? "I see. But how do you think I can help? I did talk with Ron and Martin last December. It's been almost a year." *And we removed the phone tap on Louis as soon as I reported Justin's location to Jackie.*

Clouds drifted over the sun. The northerly wind was picking up and blowing stronger. A storm was brewing. The rabbit burst out of cover and raced toward deeper brush with Leonidas in pursuit.

"Is Travis here?"

"Yes. He's down in Rodanthe installing a security system. Do you want me to call him in?"

"Anyone stalking him?" Russ laughed referring to the earlier incident at Hatteras. "I'd like to talk with him as well.

"The investigation is in contact with authorities in Toronto. One possibility we're exploring is that the body is that of Peter Dominique, an acquaintance of Mr. Lawrence."

"Oh God! Is there enough of the remains for Peter's girl friend to identify?"

"I can't go into that. I'm here to determine if you and Travis located Mr. Lawrence. His wife told us back in February she had retained you to find him. At the time there was no reason for us to look into his disappearance."

In the silence that hovered between them Alexis heard the sound of waves crashing on the beach beyond the dunes. A migrating flock of birds flew across the horizon. Clouds parted opening the way to bright November sun.

"In February, I located Justin living in a private residence on Nevis Island under the assumed name of Carter Richards. I met with him for about an hour and have had no contact since."

Quarry gone to ground, the hunter emerged from the brush covered dunes and raced exuberantly toward the porch where Alexis called to him. "Leonidas, come."